Y

Non.

Atlantis
Inbound

B. L. PROVINCIAL

FriesenPress

Suite 300 - 990 Fort St
Victoria, BC, Canada, V8V 3K2
www.friesenpress.com

ISBN
978-1-4602-8299-1 (Hardcover)
978-1-4602-8300-4 (Paperback)
978-1-4602-8301-1 (eBook)

1. Fiction, Science Fiction, Adventure

Distributed to the trade by The Ingram Book Company

Prologue

Mr. White looked across the room at the different disciplines gathered. His mind selectively picked up bits and pieces of conversation from throughout the room. It appeared that all were present; it was time to start. He climbed the stairs to the elevated portion of the floor and crossed to the centre. Stepping up, he placed both hands on top of the podium. His voice resounded, loud, clear, and concise, with a call to order.

The room fell silent; there was an air of anticipation. Mr. White started. "Each and every one of you has been working on our project for the last twelve years, so that we may succeed without any flaws.

As you are aware, one of our most esteemed members will be returning here to Atlantica. When he returns, there will be a long and arduous recovery schedule for him."

Mr. White held up his hand, pointing his index finger upward to ask his audience for a second, to give his full attention to the incoming message from his internal communication system. Speaking internally, he replied, "Mr. White here. What is so important that I need to be disturbed at this very moment?"

"This is Commander Ryan of the Vargas informing you that we will be back in Atlantica and ready to begin the Project in just over two weeks. Ryan out."

Mr. White replied, "Thank you, Commander. Have a safe journey. End transmission." For a second his thoughts went back to his friend, and to the fact that it was not every day a person travelled slightly more than one hundred million light years.

Mr. White went on speaking about some of the outstanding issues that might arise and how he needed the full efforts of all there to help in their resolution. Going through the long list on today's agenda, he could sense from the replies that things were moving along nicely. He thanked everyone for their efforts on the project, saying he would be ready for reports within the following weeks and wanted each to be complete and final. "That's all for now. Have a wonderful day!"

Mr. White closed his eyes, thinking, It will be so nice to see you again...what name did he have this time? That's right: Sam.

Chapter 1
One's Fate

The soft sounds of the alarm chime activating caused Sam to stir with a soft groan. He thought, Saturday morning...golf, that's right. He reached out his age-freckled hand without opening his eyes and pressed the snooze button.

He moaned softly. He had to get at least another ten minutes; the bed felt so warm, enveloping him in comfort and tranquility. The gentle sound of the alarm had made him forget anything he had been dreaming about. His dreams were so far and few between at this age. What was he now? That's right—he was seventy-three, though he felt, at the moment, more like fifty.

Turning over to his right side, he opened his eyes. For a moment, he wanted to look at Donna, his wife for these past forty-seven years. There was just enough light coming through the curtain-shaded window for Sam to see Donna lying on her back. A small smile formed on his lips as he looked at her flowing grey hair, half hidden by the covers. He recollected a conversation he and Donna had so very long ago.

Sam had asked Donna why she continued to keep dying her hair. He thought that the grey in her temples made her look extremely attractive and stately. Donna replied that she thought the grey just made her look old and decrepit.

But over the next several years the dye jobs became less frequent and Donna became more comfortable with her grey. He assumed that she had decided to go back to her natural colour partially because of his earlier comment, but perhaps more so because of the time and cost of getting it done.

Donna looked so peaceful sleeping. He watched her bosom rise and fall with each breath. As he looked at her, he had another recollection. He was twenty-six years old and she was twenty-three. They had dated for three years prior to getting engaged and were engaged for another year before marriage.

The reason it had taken so long for them to get married, he remembered, was himself. Donna was younger than he was and he had wanted to be sure he was actually who she wanted.

She had looked up at him, staring into his eyes. He was just over six feet tall and she was half-a-foot shorter. Her sparkling blue-eyed stare seemed to look right through him. She called him her giant, gentle soul. She always wanted to know what he was thinking about. He had been taken aback by this stare as he looked down at her then. After fifteen or twenty seconds of staring into each other's eyes, they would both smile.

A small sigh would break forth from her lips: exasperation, Sam thought, and she would punch him in the arm, laughing. "Sam, you never tell me anything. I want to know what you think; it's important to me."

Sam would laugh, stepping back and grasping his arm. "Jeez, that hurt! My arm is going numb. I'm not sure what you want from me; you know that I love you and want to spend my life at your side."

He would always remember what she said next: "Look, you big jerk, I'm not here with you because of your money." She rolled her eyes and laughed playfully. "I'm here because from the very first day we met, I felt a connection between us: a feeling that went right to my soul. I knew just shortly after you spoke to me for the first time that you were the one for me. The softness in your voice, the feeling of reassurance you emanated, told me everything I needed to know. I was never going to let you get away."

This memory came to him as readily as if the conversation had been yesterday. Neither of them had known then that Sam`s physiology would not allow for children in their lives.

Just then the alarm sounded again. Turning over to his left side, Sam reached out and turned it off. He was glad he had set the volume to low, so as not to wake Donna at 6:00 a.m. Sitting up and removing the covers, he swung his legs off the bed and placed both feet on the carpeted floor. Nathan, his best friend in the world, would be at his door within the hour.

Looking over his shoulder, he took one last look at Donna to make sure she was still sleeping. Good, he thought; he had not disturbed her.

It felt good getting out of bed this early; no day was worth wasting, sleeping it away. He rose to his full height, raised his arms over his head, and stretched. He quickly lowered them when he felt the jab in his abdomen again. "Wow, that hurt," he whispered.

Sliding his feet into his slippers, he headed off towards the bathroom to relieve himself and wash. As he took care of the tasks at hand, he thought of Nathan Cole, his best friend.

Nathan was shorter than Sam but a lot huskier; as a pair they had the looks of Abbott and Costello on a bad day. Sam and Nathan had been friends since shortly after starting to work together—on one of the larger casinos here in Vegas. Both of them were rebar workers. They constructed the wooden forms in sections, tying the rebar into a solid cage of steel or mat, ready for cement to be poured in. This work gave them the opportunity to be outside; they enjoyed the fresh air and sunshine.

That particular job had taken slightly less than a year to complete. It was during this time that they bonded as friends. On occasion, they had even put their lives in each other's' hands.

Sam knew he was at least one ahead of Nathan in the life-saving department. They kept tabs; after all, it was worth at least a few drinks and bragging rights afterwards. He remembered one such occasion vividly.

They were on the twenty-sixth floor, working along what would be the west outer wall. The cranes would lift the concrete wall panels into place and the rigging crew would secure these to the girders. Since there were no wall panels yet, Sam and Nathan, so close to the edge, had to attach their six-foot safety belt lanyards to the temporary set of cables stretching between the girders. The cables acted as railings, one at twenty-four inches above the floor and the next at forty inches. These cables ran the perimeter of the floor, preventing workers from falling to their deaths.

It was about an hour before quitting time. Sam was still slightly hung over from the celebration the night before. Nathan's wife, Claire, had given Nathan a healthy baby boy a few days earlier.

This was to be the second of three children they brought into the world. Nathan and Sam had left work the day after the birth and decided a few drinks were in order, to celebrate. Sam had asked Nathan earlier to take two to three days off to spend time with Claire and the new baby. Nathan had told him that money was in short supply at the moment and that he needed the hours to make ends meet.

After the first drink, Sam suggested that he and Donna could loan Nathan a few bucks to tide them over; they felt it was important for him to be with Claire as a family at this time. Nathan told Sam that there was just no way was he going to take their money. After all, he said, "Someone has to feed and clothe the little suckers till their eighteenth birthdays, when—God willing—they will want lives of their own away from their persecutors."

They looked at each other and burst out laughing. Sam raised his hand to the waitress, asking for another round. Well, two led to three, then who remembers? Eventually, somewhere around 1:00 a.m., Sam got Nathan back to his house and, with Claire's help, quietly laid him on the bed, knowing that they had to be at the building site at 6:00 a.m. the following morning.

They arrived on the job site just minutes apart and met up at the coffee truck. Nathan ordered black coffee for the two of them, paid the truck operator with two one-dollar bills, and told him to keep the change. Turning around, he handed Nathan a coffee. Sam reached out gently, pushing the rim of Nathan's hard hat upwards. He could see his buddy was hurting from the night before. The swollen droopy eyes tell all, Sam thought, smiling.

Nathan gave a slight smile and asked Sam to kill him. Sam laughed as he put his arm around Nathan's shoulder and led him to the temporary elevator on the outside wall of the building.

They got into the elevator with a number of other construction workers and Sam pressed the button to take them to the top floor. As the elevator ascended, he looked into Nathan's eyes and asked, "Are you going to survive the day?"

Nathan replied, "Please tell me that I didn't dance on top of any tables last night and that I still had all my clothes on when I left the bar and I think I just might." The guys in the elevator burst out laughing. Sam patted Nathan on the shoulder and said, "That's what you got me for, old buddy," and joined in the laughter.

After stopping at several lower floors to let some of the other contractors off, they finally got to the top floor, the twenty-sixth: "open sky," as they called it. They lifted the safety gate and walked off the elevator, heading for their side of the building to continue the previous day's efforts. They attached their safety lanyards to the cable railings and began to work.

Sam was surprised; even though Nathan was not feeling so hot, the work progressed at a good pace. This day, like most, they chatted about the latest news and interesting things happening around the world. They talked about the fall of the Berlin Wall, the Vietnam War, World Wars I and II, and the Cuban Missile Crisis. They agreed that men were not that bright and that someday they would blow up the world over petty squabbles.

At about 3 p.m., Nathan had to disconnect his safety lanyard to go to the porta-potty. He told Sam that nature called and that he would be back in a few. Sam watched as Nathan headed towards the john. For a few seconds, he giggled; Nathan would probably think twice about drinking so much the night before work. He chuckled to himself even harder. Not going to happen! Nathan almost seemed to enjoy starting work this way. Turning his head, Sam went back to work. Ten minutes later, he did not hear Nathan coming up behind him.

As Nathan walked toward him, he could see Sam on his knees, sideways to the edge of the floor, wiring some rebar together. He had a quick—and what turned out to be a really stupid—idea. Sam had his head down, concentrating on the job at hand. Nathan slowly and quietly snuck up behind him. When he got within two feet, he quickly reached out and jabbed Sam in the right shoulder, yelling "Boo!"

When Nathan's hand came in contact with his shoulder, Sam yelped and jumped up, twisting to his right and swinging his arm in an arc, hitting Nathan on his right side. The force of the blow caused Nathan to lose his balance and career over the cable railing, hard hat flying into open space. In a last desperate act, Nathan reached out with his gloved hand and grabbed for the cable.

It all happened so fast. Having stood up fully now, Sam continued twisting to his right. All he could do was watch as Nathan tried to grasp the top cable. Sam reached out to grab Nathan and missed by a fraction of an inch.

Fate was on Nathan's side. His hand managed to make contact with the bottom cable and closed tightly around it. The pendulum motion of his body caused him to crash against the outside of the building, bruising his ribs (as he would find out later).

Nathan screamed. Sam lunged forward and reached over the top cable, grabbing him by the collar of his shirt. Sam yelled "I got you! I won`t let go; now reach up and grab the cable with your other hand." Sam could not see Nathan's face but he knew it would be white as a ghost, as he was sure his was. Nathan grabbed the cable, groaning. With exertion on both their parts, Nathan was pulled onto the floor. Once he was safely away from the edge, the two collapsed on the floor together.

At this point, Sam lost it. He grabbed Nathan by the lapels, shaking him vigorously. "Just what the hell were you thinking?!" he screamed at Nathan. It did not help that Nathan was laughing his ass off and could make no reply. After what felt like an eternity, Sam let go of Nathan's lapels and let him fall back to the floor. Nathan was just so happy to be alive that he couldn't stop himself from laughing. When he finally sat up, he reached for Sam and gave him the biggest hug of his life. Nathan said, "I promise, from this point forward, that I will never sneak up on you again." They were both still hugging when the rest of the crew arrived on the scene.

What a memory, Sam thought as he finished dressing and headed for the kitchen to make a quick breakfast. Once there, he wasn't sure what to make himself. He had a dull, nagging pain in his lower stomach, a pain he had felt off and on again over the past several months.

"I suppose it's a good thing," he thought, "I have a doctor's appointment for my check-up on Wednesday." Ah, the heck with it, he would grab something at the golf course if he got hungry.

He heard a slight rapping. Opening the door, he saw Nathan standing in the hallway with a warm smile and a golf bag over his shoulder. Nathan now lived in the same condo building as Sam and Donna, which made it easy for them to spend time together.

Sam held his index finger to his lips, letting Nathan know to be quiet. "Good morning, buddy," he whispered, "Give me a second." After slipping his shoes on, Sam stepped into the hallway and gently closed the door. He thought to himself, Back in a few hours, sweetie. They took the elevator down to the parking garage and put Nathan's clubs in Sam's car. They got in and headed toward W. Washington Ave, just south of Fountain Park.

There were lots of golf courses in Vegas, but the majority of the new ones cost an arm and leg to play. Besides, Sam and Nathan both liked the municipal course they were going to. The course was perfect for their game: not too long or short. It had been established in 1932 and had undergone a $5 million facelift just a year ago. Between the two of them, they pretty well knew every hazard the course had. They never liked renting golf carts; they preferred to walk.

As Sam got ready to make his third shot on the second hole, a five-hundred-and-three yarder, he suddenly fell to his knees, grabbed his stomach in pain, and rolled over onto his side. Nathan ran the twenty yards to Sam. He could see that his buddy was in a great deal of pain; he was as white as his own golf glove.

Sam put his hand on Nathan's forearm and said, "I will be okay; just give me a few seconds to catch my breath." Nathan moved his hand to Sam's shoulder, squeezing it gently until he could see the colour start to come back to Sam's face and his breathing return to normal.

The twosome waiting at the tee-off behind had seen a man collapse. They jumped in their cart and made their way toward them. Helping Sam off the ground, Nathan turned and asked the twosome if he could borrow their cart to get Sam back to the clubhouse. With Sam in the passenger seat, their clubs on the roof, and Nathan standing on the back of the cart, they headed back to the clubhouse.

By the time they reached the clubhouse, Sam was pretty well back to normal; he was even laughing at how silly he must've looked. They thanked the other golfer for the use of his cart and told him that the next time they saw his party the drinks were on them. The other golfer looked at Sam before he left and said he hoped he would be okay. Nathan and Sam thanked him again as he pulled away to go back to his partner.

Nathan got their clubs into the car and asked Sam for his keys, so he could do the driving home. Sam said that he was okay but that he would let him have the keys anyway, since he was feeling a little drained.

On their way home, Sam asked Nathan not to say anything to Donna. He would tell her what had happened when the time was right. Nathan nodded his head. "Okay, Sam. When are you going to let me know what's going on?" Turning his head, Sam gave him a slight grin but said nothing.

Nathan asked Sam if he was going to go see a doctor. Sam informed Nathan that he already had a doctor's appointment set up for Wednesday. The rest of the ride home was pretty quiet, if not routine. At Sam's door, Nathan said, "Have a good day, buddy, and if you need anything, I'm just down the hall."

"Thanks," Sam replied.

It was almost 9:30 a.m. when Sam opened his condo door. His nostrils were immediately hit with the smell of maple bacon frying.

Donna hummed to herself in the kitchen. She must have heard Sam come in; she never jumped when he walked up behind her, lifted her hair to the side, and gave her a kiss on the side of the neck. Donna smiled, saying, "Would you like some?"

Sam hugged her and pulled her to him from behind, saying, in a soft low voice, "Some of what?"

She laughed and turned around, looked up at him, and replied, "Food, you big jerk. What did you think I was asking?" Sam let her go and walked over to the kitchen table. He sat down, saying softly, with a pout, "You never know if you don't ask."

"You never replied," Donna said. "Do you want some breakfast with me, or are you on a diet?"

"No thanks," Sam replied.

Donna continued frying her bacon and eggs, then opened the fridge and poured herself a glass of orange juice. Putting her food on a plate, she sat at the kitchen table across from Sam. "You're back early," she said.

Sam thought to himself, Well, I guess this is as good a time as any. He started off by saying the worst thing he could say: "I don't want you to be scared or upset."

Immediately, Donna looked up from her food, stared at Sam, and said, "Now I am scared; what's up?"

"Well, let me see," Sam said. "About four or five months ago I started to get small jabs of pain in my stomach. I've also noticed that I've been eating less; I've lost about twelve pounds. Now hold on!" he said before she could react, "I have already made a doctor's appointment for this Wednesday. I know it's a little early this year, but I'm going to ask the doctor for a complete medical workup like my yearly one, okay?"

Donna tilted her head down, placed both elbows on the table, and put her two hands over her face. Without looking at Sam, she asked, "Are you okay right now?"

Sam, still looking at her, replied that he felt just fine but went on to briefly explain what had happened on the golf course. Taking her hands away from her face, Donna looked up and asked Sam why he hadn't said anything about this pain earlier. Did she not have a right to know? Staring into her eyes, Sam could see anger building. She said, "You're damn right you're going to the doctor; I will be there with you—end of story! Now go put your clubs away and let me finish my breakfast in peace. You make me so angry at times, Sam."

Donna wondered to herself what it was about men and their need to wait till the last second to do something about a problem. Through the years of their marriage, this had been a continual issue with Sam. Sam's attitude was "Let's just wait and see if there is another solution—or maybe it will correct or repair itself." This frustrated her so much. Punching him in the arm was usually her way of letting him know that enough was enough.

She felt lucky that these little things were the only problems the two of them had, however. Sam was always there for support when she was sad. They never argued about money. They never had too much and were more often in the hole than flush, but this never endangered the relationship. Donna had seen so many marriages ruined by issues with money, booze, drugs, and anger. She and Sam had agreed at the beginning that they would not let life's little things get in the way of their happiness.

Donna gave Sam one more steely-eyed stare and then told him, "Once the clubs are put away, I think you should go spend some time with Nathan down the hall while I clean up." Sam got the message, loud and clear. Go away, you pain-in-the-ass, till I calm down. Without another word, Sam got up and slunk out of their condo unit and over to Nathan's.

Nathan invited Sam in and took one look at the huge smirking grin on Sam's face. "Kicked you out for being a moron again, eh, Mr. Stupid? When will you ever learn? What Donna sees in you, I will never understand; I don't even like you. Have a seat, my friend, and I will get you a beer." Nathan turned toward the fridge, saying, "So, how did she respond?"

Sam sat on the couch and slouched down. "About as good as I expected," he said.

Handing Sam his beer, Nathan went over to his recliner and sat down, placing his beer on the end table. "We are not getting any younger, Sam. Tell me what is going on; you have been a little distant lately." Sam's demeanour changed instantly. He proceeded to tell Nathan about the stomach issues he had experienced over the last several months. "What are you feeling inside right now, Sam?" Nathan asked.

"I am very scared right now. Hoping all will be okay with me, but with my age and the amount of pain at times, it makes it very hard not to be concerned. My biggest concern all along has been Donna." Nathan could see the glistening of tears in his friend's eyes and for the first time realized that Sam was really scared about this. Now Nathan was afraid too.

Nathan decided to try to lighten things up a bit. "So here we are, two old farts sitting and talking about our feelings and getting all teary-eyed. I hope none of our guy buddies see us now; they would have a field day and make us pay dearly for losing our manhood." The two of them started to laugh out loud at the silliness of it all.

After several minutes of laughing and feeling the tension in the room subside, Sam added, "They would probably go out and buy us man purses, and have both of us walk down the street with them on our shoulders." This brought on a whole lot more laughter. "Okay, okay, I feel better now," Sam said. "I hope you realize you are not helping my stomach pain right now, though, buddy boy."

"Without getting ahead of ourselves, let's just wait and see what the doctor has to say," Nathan said.

Sam stated, "We have been through so much together over the years. I'm so glad we became friends." Nathan picked up his beer and moved it toward Sam in a toasting motion; they touched beer bottles.

Nathan said, "Ditto, buddy. Enough of this girly talk. Go home to your wife; you know, the one who just kicked you out." The two of them smiled at each other, then chugged down the rest of their beers.

During the few days leading up to the doctor's appointment, Donna kept Sam busy doing chores around the condo. They had lived there for the past ten years, since selling their house at the north end of the city. They lived far enough away from the airport not to be bothered by the sounds of the countless planes coming and going every hour of the day and night. Sam knew the condo was a good choice for them now that they weren't getting any younger.

From their eighteenth-floor balcony, they could look over the city below and see the casinos and mountains off in the distance. Sam also had his telescope set up here. He had always been fascinated by the night sky. His father had started him on this hobby when he was around twelve years old. They would stay out in their backyard for hours some evenings, his dad giving him pointers on focusing the telescope and understanding the starry heavens above. At times, as he looked out at the various celestial bodies, Sam wished he had the ability to travel among them and see the wonders they held.

As he had become more familiar with the stars, he had also become aware of the distances between them: so enormous. He and his father would speculate about the idea of other life evolving out there. Would any life forms be friendly or war-like? Would they look like humans or more insect-like?

Sam's father had always treated Sam with respect and tried to answer his questions by letting Sam know that he was only telling Sam what he believed were the correct answers. If Sam was not sure of the answers his father gave, he was told to look up his questions at the library. Many times, Sam remembered coming back from the library with different answers than those his father had given him. His father would just smile and tell Sam, "You always have to remember the answers I give you are based on what I know or believe to be right. When you go to the library and find a different answer, it is also only the opinion of another person."

Sam's father told him, "No one really knows what is out there in space. We just try to learn and understand all we can from the information at hand. In the scheme of things, our understanding is so tiny compared to the vastness of the universe and all its wonders. Most times all we can do is speculate and dream.

"Someday, Sam, man will travel the stars and discover more of the truth for himself and humanity. This is how we humans learn to organize our thoughts and daily lives, one step at a time. There is no such thing as a wrong answer, just one that does not meet our beliefs at the time." Sam was not sure he understood all of this. Over time, he discovered for himself that his father was mostly correct.

Six years ago, Nathan had moved into the condo unit just down the hall from them. They had all taken it badly when Claire died in a car accident some seven years ago. Nathan stayed in his house for just over a year afterward. It got too big and empty for him after that, with the kids hardly coming home any more. Two were married and had lives of their own; the third and youngest was off somewhere trying to save the planet, Greenpeace or some other organization like that. Donna had informed Nathan that there was an empty condo near them, and he moved in shortly after. The three of them usually got together twice a week for supper and a little TV. Nathan had shown no real interest in female companionship. He had gone out on a few dates but never got attached to another woman.

●

●   ●

None of the tasks Sam undertook that week were hard or time-consuming. A screw here, a nail there. He changed several light bulbs and cleaned the filters for the portable air-cleaning unit. Now and again Sam would feel stomach pain, shrug it off, and continue his work. The pain was not nearly as strong as it had been on the golf course, but add in the indigestion he was having and he wasn't a happy camper.

Wednesday finally came. Sam awoke at 7:00 a.m. sharp without the alarm clock, as he did every day. He went over to the window and pulled open the curtain just enough to see what the day was going to be like. Their bedroom window faced northwest toward the mountains. From this vantage point he could see any bad weather coming in over the mountains. "Well," he said to himself, "looks like another beautiful sunshine-filled day in Vegas."

He and Donna both loved living here. It was sunny ninety percent of the time. Between the middle of October and the end of March, it hovered around sixty to eighty-five degrees Fahrenheit. In the summer, when the temperature got over a hundred, he pretty much stayed around the condo: no golfing, just going in and out to get the essentials.

Vegas was where he and Donna had met so long ago. He worked in construction at the time and she worked as a waitress in a restaurant he frequented for supper. He was young, single, had a good job, and made really good money. He couldn't be bothered with cooking at his apartment, other than a snack now and again.

Chapter 2
Reality

Sam went into the kitchen and set up and turned on the coffee machine, then turned and headed for the washroom. After getting undressed, he stepped into the shower feeling good, knowing that the coffee would be ready when he was finished. The water cascaded over his body. "Man, this is so nice," he whispered. After showering and shaving, Sam took his clothes out and proceeded to get dressed. The alarm clock on the nightstand showed 7:55 a.m.

He walked over to the bed on Donna's side, bent over, gave her a peck on the forehead, and nudged her gently, saying, "Hey, sweetie, eight o'clock. It's time to get up."

Donna stirred slowly, opened her eyes, and looked up, saying a real soft "Hi." Knowing it would take her at least forty minutes to show up in the kitchen, Sam left and started on his first coffee.

He was halfway into his second cup when Donna walked in, saying, "It looks like it's going to be a nice day!" Sitting there over the next half hour, they talked about the day ahead: the doctor's appointment and the shopping to do afterwards.

It took a little less than half an hour to reach Mountain Valley Clinic and park. As they approached the main entrance, a young man held the door open for them. Sam thanked him and walked into the clinic behind Donna. It was a short walk to the bank of elevators. As Sam pressed the button to go up, he felt a small jab in his stomach. Not giving any indication to Donna, he gritted his teeth, stood straight, and put his hands in his pockets.

The elevator doors opened and several people, including a few nurses, got off. He and Donna got in; Donna pressed the button for the sixth floor and they watched the doors close. Looking down at his watch, Sam saw that they were about fifteen minutes early. They got out of the elevator on the sixth floor, made a right, and headed down the hallway to room 6322, Dr. Harvey's office.

Entering the sitting area, Sam helped Donna to a chair then headed to the receptionist's desk. He introduced himself and gave the time of his appointment to the receptionist. Taking her pen, she skimmed down the list to his name: Sam White. She checked it off and asked him to please take a seat; it would only be a few moments.

A half hour later, he was called into Dr. Harvey's office. The office wasn't opulent: two chairs in front of a small steel desk, a four-drawer filing cabinet, scattered posters of various diseases on the wall, and a door leading to the examination room. After they were seated, the doctor looked up, smiled, and asked Sam what he could do for him today.

Not knowing where to start, Sam blurted out that he had sharp pains in his stomach and heartburn like crazy and was losing weight. He was asked how long he had been feeling the pains and, on a number from one to ten (ten being excruciating), what their severity was. Sam told the doctor that the pain had started about five months earlier and had been getting stronger since then. The last one he had, he said, was probably around an eight. Dr. Harvey asked if the indigestion had also been present for five months. Sam replied, "Yes, I think so."

The doctor, still looking at Sam, said, "Why don't we step into the examination room and I'll have a closer look." In they went, closing the door behind them. Fifteen minutes later, they came out and sat in their respective chairs. Without saying a word, Dr. Harvey opened his drawer, pulled out his lab pad, and started to write. When he finished checking off the various test boxes and signing the bottom, he turned the note around toward Sam and went through the tests he wanted Sam to have.

He told Sam that he should have a gastroscopy. This test involved Sam being put under and a fiber-optic camera sent into his stomach so that the doctors could have a better look. After that, he wanted Sam to have a Computed Tomography (CT) scan of his stomach area. This test would tell them if there were any problems in the adjacent tissues.

Looking at Donna, the doctor could see that she was upset. Dr. Harvey told the two of them that they should not worry at this stage; these tests were routine for the symptoms. Smiling now, Sam and Donna got up, shook the doctor's hand, and thanked him for his time. They walked out of the office, went down the elevator, and got in the car. Sam looked at Donna. "Oh boy, now we can go shopping." They both laughed.

The doctor's office phoned later in the day and said they were able to get Sam in for the gastroscopy on Friday of this week and the CT on Monday of next week, both at Mount Charleston Hospital, just down the road. Sam thought that he was getting these exams very quickly compared to his previous experiences with medical tests. Did he have something to really worry about?

●

●　　　　　　●

The rest of the week and the weekend came and went quickly. Donna and Sam went to the scheduled appointments. The tests were completed and all that was left was to wait for the results. During this time, Donna and Sam pondered the tests and their outcome. Mostly they kept their thoughts to themselves, trying to stay as positive as possible in front of each other.

Donna's thoughts seemed to rally around Sam's anxiety as the cause of the indigestion and pain. She didn't really believe this inwardly, however, because with Sam retired now and taking life at such a leisurely pace, there were really no signs of stress. Sam, on the other hand, though he had been healthy for most of his life, was more of a mind to think the worst. In this way, he thought, when everything came back negative, he would feel total relief.

They received a call from the doctor's office early one morning, a week and a half later. Dr. Harvey's receptionist asked Sam to return to the clinic to speak with the doctor about his results. An appointment was set up for the following day. There was never a choice for Sam to see the doctor on his own; Donna made it very clear that she was going to be with him. Sam accepted her choice reluctantly, but with the understanding that she wanted to support him and make sure he went.

At 10:00 a.m. sharp on Friday morning, Sam and Donna sat in the doctor's office. They watched as Dr. Harvey walked in, folder in his left hand. He shook their hands and sat behind his desk. Dr. Harvey, they could both see, was taking his time, choosing his words carefully before he spoke. "Good morning," he said, breaking the silence. "I have to assume you both know the reason you were called here today. The tests came back showing a problem. I would like to lay out what the issues are and explain where we go from here. The gastroscopy results revealed a medium-sized mass on the inside lining of your stomach. We did a biopsy on this mass to check for cancer cells. As it turns out, it was identified as gastric cancer."

Donna looked at Dr. Harvey and asked, before Sam could, just how serious this was and whether it could be taken care of with an operation. Dr. Harvey held up his hand, asking her to please listen to the rest of the report first. Afterward, he would take all the time necessary to answer questions to their satisfaction. He understood her wanting to know immediately. "What I want to do," he said, "is give you a complete picture of the prognosis and the procedures moving forward.

"The possibility of this diagnosis is why, after the gastroscopy exam, I believed it would be prudent to follow up with a CT scan. This scan is also used to detect cancer but is more useful in determining if the cancer has invaded adjacent tissues or lymph nodes. Gastric cancer is usually at an advanced stage by the time it is diagnosed. This means it has metastasized to the other organs already. I am sorry if you think I am coming across as cold, but it is better to be clear and know where you stand, Sam."

"And exactly where is that?" Sam reluctantly asked.

"In my career, I have had to be the bearer of bad news to many of my patients and I want you to know that it has never been easy to tell them—or you—the outcome ahead." Dr. Harvey could see tears streaming down Donna's cheeks. He reached out and passed her a tissue box.

After taking several tissues, wiping her eyes, and dabbing her nose, Donna sat up straighter. Gathering her strength, she weakly asked, "Are you trying to say Sam is going to die?" Reaching over, Sam placed his hand on Donna's shoulder. It was a reflex; his own mind tried to grasp the message it was receiving.

Dr. Harvey decided it was time for the final truth. Bringing his hands together in front of him and joining the tips of his fingers and his thumbs in the shape of a cathedral, he said, "With this form of cancer in the late stage it is in, there is only a fifteen-percent chance—or less—of survival. We can perform an operation and remove the part of the stomach affected, along with the surrounding lymph nodes." Dr. Harvey added, "With this procedure we could possibly prolong your life for weeks, at best. We can also introduce chemotherapy with radiation but all this will do is slow the inevitable."

Gathering every bit of strength he could muster, Sam was able to get out five words: "How long do I have?"

"In my opinion, and you can get a second one if you wish, Sam, you have approximately four to six months at the most."

The rest of the appointment was spent discussing the pros and cons of every possible avenue. The end result would remain the same. The next several months would be very painful and come very quickly. Dr. Harvey would prescribe medications to ease the physical pain. The psychological part would not be so easy. Dr. Harvey apologized again for being the bearer of bad news and told them his door was open and his phone available at any time of the day or night for further questions.

The following days and weeks passed in a blur. Sam did not want operations or radiation of any kind in the time he had left. He spoke with Donna and she understood. Full comprehension took a long time to sink in. The next stage was the depression of knowing roughly when you were going to die. After this, there was anger at God and everyone else, for just being, for having the ability to live on when he could not. Finally came the realization and understanding that each of us has our time. It is how we greet Death that makes us who we are.

There was never a second that Sam contemplated suicide; it wasn't an option for him. He told himself he would face the end of his existence with the poise and grace it had taken him a lifetime to develop. He would sit and philosophize to himself, with statements like, "When your time comes, it comes."

As time went by, and with the help of the pain medications, Sam took more time for himself. Most of all, he asked himself if his contributions, in this life, to his loved ones and those around him met his own sense of perfection.

Sam did not like to think that he had no control over his future. And, though he had not gone to church often or prayed much, he still wanted to believe in some form of afterlife. Which form this new life would take, he had no idea. However, more often than not, this belief seemed to bring a sense of equilibrium to his life. The thoughts of a beginning and an end stayed in check, balancing each other and preventing his mind from wandering too far.

During this time of confusion and fear, Sam and Nathan spent more time together, either at his condo or Nathan's, depending on the subjects to be discussed. The last thing Sam wanted to do was depress Donna any more than she was already.

Sam often went by himself to Nathan's condo, allowing himself precious moments away from Donna and from having to see the fear in her eyes. In one of their conversations, Nathan asked Sam if he was afraid of dying. Sam's only reply was, "No, not really, not anymore. I truly believe when the end comes my mind and my body will tell me they are tired, so tired it will be time to sleep."

Sitting with Nathan and talking about old times and all the things they had done together, the friendship and the love each held for the other, helped Sam cope with what was to come. He always went back to his condo more relaxed and able to deal with Donna's sadness and his own. Trying to manage Donna's grief in these last few months was harder on Sam than he ever imagined. Her eyes seemed to lose their sparkle. He could feel the fatigue emanating from her body when they held each other close. With all his heart he wished for a magic potion to take her sadness away.

On several occasions, Sam and Donna discussed the possibility of their joining afterwards in heaven. One time she jokingly told him that he would probably be burned and blinded by the bright light and the gate would be locked when he tried to cross over. They both laughed, this relieved of a world of tension, at least for the moment.

After four and a half months, the painkillers were no longer working and Sam was too weak to help himself in even the small-est way. His weight loss was escalating at a feverish pace. Sam was taken by ambulance to Mount Charleston Hospital, where he was put in the ICU on oxygen and a multitude of pain-reducing drugs.

Nathan visited several times, as did a few of his buddies from the golf club. For some reason, it seemed to fall on Sam to make the visitors comfortable with his illness and its outcome. He was still the same Sam that they always knew; he had no more control over the illness or its outcome than they did. He just wanted to be treated normally. Sam could not always remember who came and went; the drugs he was kept on dulled his pain and mind most of the time.

Several times, over this period in the hospital, while he still had most of his mental faculties, he would make Donna leave and get some rest. If she had her way, she would be with him in bed, holding him, twenty-four hours a day.

At the end, Sam thought of how tired he really was: beyond comprehension. Fatigue filled every ounce of his being. As his mind faded to darkness, his body became totally relaxed. His second-to-last thought was of his conversation with Nathan about the tiredness. The last thought was a mumbled, I love you, my wife. I need to rest now. Darkness, no light!

Chapter 3
New Beginnings

Opening his eyes, or what he thought were his eyes, Sam kept very still. It was taking some time for his vision to clear. He knew he was standing. Off to his left, out of reach, he could sense a presence. His perception was that this presence was neither good nor bad. Not knowing where he was or what was going on, Sam was frightened and filled with anxiety.

Suddenly, a flood of memories came to his mind. They seemed all jumbled, disjointed, running at a pace that his mind could not keep up with. Feelings of love, pain, bewilderment, heartache, and longing flashed together. The feelings were so strong—too much too fast. With all his energy, he tried to push them away. Sam had to force his mind to slow down and go one step at a time.

Dying! The memory flooded his mind. This was the memory that sat on top of all the others; it was the one he had to first understand. Sam knew this one would help the other jumbled memories fall into place. His mind raced to find the answer, but there was nothing, just a blur of emotions, nothing coherent. Sam's vision started to clear. He turned his head slowly to the left, letting his gaze take in some of his surroundings. He focused on the ceiling above; it seemed to glow with a diffused light. There were no tiles, no cross members; the ceiling seemed to be all light. Strange was the only word to come to mind.

His eyes focused on a man, standing against the far wall to his left. The man's hair was pure white, not grey, cascading down both sides of his head and over his broad shoulders almost to his overlapped hands, which were placed in front of his body. His feet were encased in white sandals. His slacks were white and perfectly creased under an impressive three-quarter-length white jacket unbuttoned in the front. Under the jacket was a bright red shirt with no collar.

Most outstanding was the man's face: clear aquamarine eyes sparkling with life, a broad forehead, square nose, and wide curved lips. His skin was like that of a man who lived in the Sunbelt: heavily tanned. He emanated an air of confidence and tranquility.

Sam cleared his throat, then asked, "Who are you and where am I?"

The man gave Sam a slight smile, showing just a hint of perfect teeth. "Sam," he said, "My name is Mr. White. For the next little bit, I would like you to stay where you are, facing me. Only look at me, nothing else. Not up or down, not left or right. Can you do this for me, Sam?"

"I can," Sam replied, though he was not really sure why. This man's voice sounded so smooth and reassuring. Sam needed the calm; he needed his mind to only focus on one thing at a time right now. He stared into Mr. White's eyes.

After a few more seconds, Mr. White said, "As to where you are, all I can tell you at this time is: you are here! I know this is not a very good answer—or at least not the one you wanted. Please, let me continue!" Mr. White went on. "Let's deal with just a few facts to start with and see where they take us, okay?"

"Alright," Sam reluctantly replied. After what seemed like an eternity, Mr. White said, "Yes, Sam, you died. Yes, there is an afterlife. Without looking at yourself, staring right at me only, how do these facts make you feel?"

"To be honest," Sam replied, "I always felt inside myself there was something afterwards. I'm very scared right now, to say the least, but I also have a feeling of relief." Sam then asked Mr. White if he was God.

With a smile, Mr. White said, "No, I am not God, not even an apostle, and I will go one step further and tell you this is neither heaven nor hell. Sam, have you ever known someone who lost an arm or a leg in an accident?"

This question threw a curve ball Sam's way; he wondered what it had to do with his situation. "Yes," Sam replied, "One of my co-workers from Vegas lost an arm from the elbow down. He was hospitalized for weeks. Why?"

"Sam, do you remember that for the longest time after his accident your friend said he could still feel his arm and fingers, like they were still there?"

"Right, I remember now; he told me how itchy his fingers got at times."

"Okay, hold that thought for a second, Sam." After a short pause, Mr. White said, "All living things have what is called an aura surrounding their entire bodies. This aura is made up of electromagnetic energy. Have you heard of this, Sam?" Sam replied that he had, a long time ago, and that this aura could not be seen by the naked eye. Mr. White smiled. "Correct. Did you also know it contains the essence, the life force, if you will, of what it surrounds?"

"No. I thought it might just be heat waves emanating from an object," Sam replied.

"Well, now you have learned differently," Mr. White said. Sam realized that this conversation fascinated him and also helped to clear the confusion from some of his thoughts, making them slightly less important for the time being.

"For today, I would like to expand on this information just a little more. Is this okay with you, Sam?" Sam nodded slowly. "Okay, let's proceed," Mr. White stated. "This aura exists around the body from its beginning. No two auras are the same. There are three electromagnetic fields that make up an aura, each with its own frequency or color; these fields are interrelated. It is the interaction between them that creates each person's—or organic object's—specific aura.

"The colors of one's aura change all the time. Auras change shape and color, or a combination of both, based on emotions, physical health, and imagination. In your friend's situation, the arm was gone but the aura's electromagnetic energy continued for months or years afterward before re-conforming to the new shape of its host's body. This is why he could still feel the missing parts. Does this make sense to you, Sam?"

"It is starting to now," Sam responded. Mr. White, without hesitation, walked over to Sam, stopped three feet in front of him, and reached out his hand as if to shake Sam's. Without thinking, Sam reached for the offered hand. He was shocked not to see his own hand and arm make contact with Mr. White's. The surprise of realizing that his hand was not visible caused Sam to retreat backwards like a bolt of lightning. Falling on his ass, he slid back the last two feet to the wall, striking it quite hard. Looking down, Sam could not see his legs, either. He blurted a startled question, asking Mr. White just what in the hell was going on.

Coming to his aid, Mr. White knelt down in front of Sam. "I hope you are not too upset with me for tricking you into seeing—or, should I say, not seeing—the transformation stage you are presently in?"

Eyes darting back and forth, trying to see his arms and legs, Sam asked if this was how he was going to always be. Mr. White replied, "Not at all, Sam. You are just in the aura phase. Your physical form does not exist. It was left on Earth." Mr. White went on, "One thing you need to know is that the physical form an individual has is only present for the use of others. It is in this way that other beings can interact with you. The physical form allows beings to recognize, feel, smell, and bond with one another.

"Sam," Mr. White continued, "it is this physical form which wears out over time and dies. No one has control over the degradation of the physical body. Since forever it has been this way. We have tried to extend physical life medically but have only managed to extend it for several hundred years. With the use of micro-nano-technology we can extend it for up to a few thousand years. Beyond this, we have the ability to clone a person over and over. The aura without a body will only survive for a short period. Before the aura dissipates totally, it must be revitalized. This process will be explained later."

Without speaking, Sam held up his right hand to stop Mr. White from saying any more. Mr. White stood up and took a few steps backwards, giving space for Sam to also stand. Rising, Sam looked at Mr. White and told him that his mind could not absorb any more at this time. Mr. White assured Sam that he understood and would leave Sam by himself until later. Turning, Mr. White proceeded toward the doorway, where he swiped his hand across a small lighted panel on the right side. The door vanished from sight instantly, allowing Sam a glimpse of the corridor beyond. Within seconds of Mr. White's departure, the door rematerialized as a solid object.

The room, by Sam's best guess, was about fifteen feet square. There were no pictures on the cream-coloured walls but there was a kiosk-like device built into one wall and four small alcoves. Each one had a small lighted panel above it. The alcoves were of different sizes, ranging from about six to twenty square inches. All were approximately twenty inches deep. In the farthest left-hand corner, away from the door, was a clear, dimly lit four-foot square panel, flush to the floor. To Sam, it looked like a pad one would stand on. Maybe it was a version of a shower? There were no taps or sprinkler heads, though. There were no buttons on the wall beside or near it. Turning his gaze toward the other corner, he noticed a bed, with a thin mattress and pillow. In the middle of the room a twenty-four-inch cylindrical column stood, about three feet tall, with two other shorter and smaller cylinders on each side. Sam assumed that the larger one was a table and the two shorter ones chairs. It all looked very futuristic to him. Walking over to the table, he sat down on one of the smaller columns.

Sam allowed his conversation with Mr. White to come to the forefront of his thoughts. He did die; this he accepted. There could be no other explanation for how he now looked and the strangeness of his surroundings. With this acknowledgment came memories of his previous life. In a blur of images, he saw parts of his life unfold in chronological order. He remembered his mother's kisses and his father's hugs. He remembered always finding their loving arms to hold him when he was sick or hurting. The times his father would teach him something new about life and its rewards. He remembered the pain of watching them both die, the feeling of being alone and how empty he felt after the death of each. He recalled his first date with Donna, their marriage, and finding out they could not have children together. The problem was with him, not her. Sam knew the sorrow Donna felt over this, though she always smiled and said it was meant to be. She told Sam she was happy as long as they had each other. There were memories of his friendship with Nathan and Claire and all the good and bad times they had shared.

At this point, his last moments with Donna flashed into his mind. The memory of her sitting at his bedside holding and squeezing his hands with hers. She was telling him how much she loved him and how happy she was to have had a lifetime of wonderful memories by his side. She said she could see how tired he was and that it was time for him to let go and rest. This last part was said with tears flowing down her cheeks onto their held hands. Sam's last thought was of her thanking him for always being so good to her but telling him that it was time for her not to be selfish and to let him go. Sam knew it would be a long time before he would start to feel the emotional pain from these memories subside.

He reached up with his fingers to wipe away the tears running down his cheeks. He could feel a slight physical resistance when his fingers touched his cheeks even though he could not see his hands. Thinking for a second, he figured the resistance came from one part of his aura coming in contact with itself. He giggled to himself at this; was he already starting to accept what was happening and rationalizing it?

Sam reached out his hand, palm down, and slowly lowered it to the table's surface. At about three inches, he started to feel resistance, but it was not the same as when he touched his cheek; it seemed cooler. Going back and forth a few times with his hand from table to cheek, he became familiar with the slight variation. Standing up and going over to the wall, the door, and the bed, he tried the same experiment and got the same results; non-living objects had a cooler feel and less resistance. During these tests he wondered why his hand could not pass through the different objects. He would have to ask Mr. White about this.

Physically, Sam felt good: younger, more flexible and agile than he remembered feeling for a long time. One thing surprised him; he did not feel physically fatigued. Even with all the stress of his new location and form and the loss of his old life, he felt strong, somewhat invigorated. Though he was confused about what was happening, Sam liked the feeling.

He thought, "This room is boring, so quiet, nothing to do or see." He walked over to the door and swiped his hand across the lighted panel; the lights flashed for a millisecond then went back to their original color. The door did not disappear. Immediately his mind went to thoughts of being a captive. But why? For what reason?

Turning quickly, he went to the other panels and swiped his hand across them with the same results: nothing! He walked over to the lighted pad in the corner, stepped on it, waited, and jumped up and down. Still nothing. "What is going on here?" he said out loud. There was no response to this, either. Just as he gave up and walked over to sit on the bed, the door vanished and there stood Mr. White.

Mr. White smiled, then lifted his hand, motioning for Sam to come with him. He said, "Would you like to go for a stroll with me, Sam?"

Cautiously walking over to the open door and Mr. White, Sam replied, "Yes, that would be nice; I was starting to feel claustrophobic."

Upon walking out the door, the first thing Sam noticed was how far the corridor went in both directions. They turned right. Along each wall of the passageway there were what had to be several hundred other doors on both sides. The corridor was lit from the ceiling in the same way as his room. It was hard to judge the height of the ceiling: perhaps twelve feet? The walls were of the same material as his room; it looked like a hard plastic without a sheen, duller. The floor had a shiny polished look, like marble but not of any color he had ever seen. It was almost baby blue, with a hint of green.

As the two of them proceeded silently along the hallway, Sam saw the space open up into a much larger area ahead. As they walked into this area, Sam noticed floor-to-ceiling windows on one side.

The room was scattered here and there with sitting areas consisting of four armchairs each, all looking very comfortable. In the middle of each of these areas was a small, oval-shaped, solid-looking coffee table.

Leaving Mr. White's side, curious to see the view outside, Sam walked toward one of the floor-to-ceiling windows. The distance to the window was about sixty paces. The closer Sam got, the greater the sense of height he felt above the outside surroundings. Upon arriving at the window, Sam saw they were very high above street level. Looking out across the buildings in front of and below him, he could see the city went on and on, all the way to the horizon.

Many flying objects travelled in all directions. Some were huge and slow while others were small and flew swiftly. Most were flying lower from this view, only a few higher. Sam stood silently, in awe at the size and scope of the landscape. He could see hundreds of skyscraper-sized structures. It looked to Sam as if the city was laid out in concentric circles; his building seemed to be in the centre. As the circles got farther out, the structures got higher. This could just be an illusion, he thought, but the city is obviously massive.

Looking upward toward the sky, Sam saw blue and wisps of cloud. The view of several large moons caught his eye almost immediately. He could count three, all of different sizes. Since it was daytime, the moons in the distance were almost opaque. They gave the landscape a sci-fi appearance; none of it seemed real at all. With a sound that was almost a giggle, Sam whispered to himself, "Well, Dad, it looks like you were right."

Just then, Mr. White asked Sam to come sit with him so they could chat some more. Turning his attention away from the window, Sam went over to where Mr. White was sitting and sat down across from him. "Do you have any questions for me?" Mr. White asked.

"I have hundreds," Sam relied. "I am not sure just where to start." Pausing for a few seconds, Sam gathered his thoughts. "Let's start with, 'Who are you, and why am I here?'"

Mr. White smiled softly. "I am the one who will guide you for the next several weeks and explain to you all the things you need to know. I am only one of many Mr. Whites here on Atlantica."

Sam looked at Mr. White and asked him, "If there are many of you, does this mean you are a clone?"

Mr. White responded, "To be cloned, I would have to be biological in nature. I am not. I am more...how shall I put this so you can understand?"

"A robot," Sam said.

Laughing now, Mr. White went on, "I go far beyond your comprehension of a robot. I am made up of mechanical organs and a soft rubber-like polymer skin, with a central nervous system similar to your own. In this way, I can duplicate all your senses. My brain is made up of trillions of liquid-organic microchips; each one is mechanical but also living matter. My chips work together just like your brain's neurons, which giving you memories, thoughts, feelings, and emotions. I was made as close to human specifications as possible. Can you grasp this concept, Sam?"

"I think so," Sam replied, "but let me rephrase it in my own way, to help my brain to accept what you're saying."

"Okay," Mr. White said.

Sam said, "For all intents and purposes, you are not human, but you have the ability to mimic all that is human, and you can live forever?"

Mr. White responded with a nod of his head. "Yes, that pretty much sums it up, Sam. The main difference is that I do not have all the freedom of choice that you have. I serve a collection of purposes which are programmed into me; these give me my direction."

Jumping on this statement, Sam asked, "So, someone or something else controls you?"

"Yes, this is true, Sam, but even I don't know the whos or whys. I am just happy to be a part of all this around us."

"I guess," Sam said, "this is another area in which we are different. I need to know the reasons why I do things and how my choices will affect me."

Mr. White said, "Sam, we look at the greater good our being does and we are satisfied with our direction."

"Okay, so where are we now and how long did it take to get wherever here is?" Sam asked.

"We are approximately one hundred million light years from your Earth, and it took us two and a half months to bring you here."

Sam sat back, saying, "I cannot even grasp that distance. How it is possible to have gotten so far in so little time? When I was growing up, my father told me how the stars we saw were only a part of our galaxy and that the Milky Way is about seventy thousand light years across. What my dad told me, and everything I learned later, let me know that man would be lucky to explore even a small portion of our own galaxy in the next thousand years. Now you are talking about millions of light years. How? And why are you using all the terms we use on Earth for everything? Is it so I will understand you better?"

"I was wondering how long it would take you to ask me about my terminology," Mr. White said. "You see, Sam, everything is relevant. By this I mean that the terms we use are the same terms used throughout the universe. Technologies are different. Languages are different, but only by degrees or, shall I say, perspective. Over the next several weeks you will learn more about this issue and will see how the universe as you know it is a community. This is all I can say right now. Anyway, back to your question of how we got you here so fast."

Mr. White asked Sam, "What have you heard about deep space travel and how to achieve it?"

"Well," Sam said, "I have heard the terms 'warp drive,' and 'folding space,' and read about the cosmic acceleration theory."

Mr. White nodded. "Those are all hypothetical terms, Sam; the only use they have is in science fiction. Can you imagine what would happen if you tried to fold space, Sam? The catastrophic events that would take place as millions of solid bodies came in contact with each other? The universe would be destroyed. Anyway, any applications of those ideas would never achieve the speeds needed for reaching other galaxies."

"So, tell me then, how have you managed to do it?" Sam asked.

Across the room, Sam noticed another Mr. White entering the sitting area. This Mr. White talked and gestured with his hands as if he was saying something to someone who was not there. He proceeded to another sitting area about eighty feet away and sat down, still talking. Sam asked his Mr. White, "Why is he talking to himself?"

"He is speaking to someone just like you, Sam, someone in their aura phase." Sam sat back in his chair trying to see this other being: nothing. He gave up and turned his attention back to his Mr. White. "It is as I told you earlier, Sam; you cannot see another's aura."

"I was wondering if I was all alone on this floor. I have seen no one else, but I guess this answers my question," Sam stated.

"You are not alone here, Sam. At this time, there are one million and forty-seven people in the aura phase in this building."

Sam stared at Mr. White in awe. "You are telling me that there are more than a million people in this building? Just how big is this structure?"

Mr. White responded, "This one building has 1360 floors and is about three miles square. This is one of our smaller buildings. You did notice when you looked outside that the buildings get much taller as you look further out?"

Sam asked, "How can you construct buildings so large without them collapsing under their own weight?"

Mr. White replied that the materials used were ten thousand times stronger and lighter than those used on Earth. "Do you know how many elements there are in your periodic table?"

Sam thought for a minute, then said, "I think it is about 120 or so."

"Well, here we know of 236 and we have a fuller understanding of how to use and combine those elements to a very high degree."

Momentarily straying from their conversation, Sam asked when he would get out of this phase and back into solid form so he could eat again.

"We keep you in this phase for a few weeks to make sure your aura's rings are stable and cohesive. You do not require food in this phase. We are supplying you with dark matter energy to sustain you; you should not feel hunger. After this process, we will take you to the renormalization lab across the city, where your new body will be created." Mr. White said, "Just before you are taken to the lab, you will be given a choice. I will discuss this and other subjects with you tomorrow morning, Sam. For the rest of this evening, I would like you to enjoy this area. In the mean time I have given you access to enter and leave your room, and to go to the lounge area only. When you get tired, please return to your room for the night. I will leave you alone now." Standing up, Mr. White turned to walk away and then stopped. He turned back to Sam and asked him not to try to speak to the other Mr. White. "He would not acknowledge you, anyway. Goodnight, Sam," he said, and walked away.

Getting to his feet, Sam started to giggle softly. Not in his wildest dreams did he ever imagine the afterlife being this way. The stories he could tell Donna and Nathan, even from just the little he seen so far... Wow, he thought. Walking to the same window as before, he imagined that he had his arm around Donna's waist and they were both looking at the scene laid out before them. He missed her so much! Looking toward the three moons in the sky above, Sam softly whispered, "I am not sure what lies ahead for me, but you will always have my heart, Donna. Sweet dreams, my love!"

Going back down the long hallway, Sam found his room easily. When he walked out of the hall and entered the corridor, a small light on a wall panel flashed, and down the hallway he noticed a door light up and blink slowly. This must be his room. As soon as he entered the room, the door rematerialized, closing him in. He was very tired and lay quietly on the bed, waiting for sleep to overtake him.

• • •

At what seemed very early the next morning, a gentle buzzing sound came from the direction of the door. Rising from his bed, Sam stood up and stretched. He smiled and a sense of well-being took hold of him as he remembered the pain he use to have stretching first thing every morning. Lowering his invisible arms, Sam called out, "Come in."

The door promptly vanished and he saw Mr. White standing in the hallway, framed by the door. "Good morning, Sam. I hope you slept well," Mr. White said.

"Yes, I did, thank you," Sam replied.

Smiling at Sam and turning left, facing down the hall, Mr. White asked Sam to please join him again in a walk to the Lounge at the end of the hall. Sam replied "Sure," and walked out to accompany his mentor. Entering the room, they made their way over to the same place as yesterday and sat down opposite each other.

After what seemed like minutes had passed, Mr. White said, "Today you will learn of your past: your accomplishments, your mistakes, and also your regrets. Today you will have many more of your beliefs quashed. You will learn things about yourself that will both astonish and dismay you." Not stopping to let Sam reply, he went on to tell Sam how he would be repulsed by some things of his own doing. He was going to tell Sam about Sam! Sitting back now, Mr. White waited for a response.

Gathering his thoughts slowly, Sam told Mr. White that he was aware of all the things he had done in his life and how a person does not live for seventy-three years and not have some regrets and thoughts of remorse. "I am not as concerned about your past seventy-three years as I am about your past thirty-six hundred years," Mr. White stated.

Jaw dropping, eyes widening, Sam sat back softly. "What! Thirty-six hundred years? What are you talking about?"

31

"Sam, you were originally born in the year 1589 BC, in the land of Goshen, which was ruled by the Egyptians and pharaohs."

"How can this be?" Sam said incredulously. "You said yourself that the body of a man can only be kept alive for a few hundred years." Mr. White leaned forward and told Sam he was happy he had been listening to their earlier talk.

"Over the past thirty-six hundred years, your aura has been returned to Atlantica every time your physical body expired, just like this time. Overall, Sam, you have lived a total of one-hundred-and-twenty-seven lifetimes, with an average life span of thirty-eight years. Let me go on to say that many of those lifetimes were begun with memories of past lives intact and several were started from scratch, meaning that you were reborn as a baby with no memory. If you do the math, you will see that these numbers do not add up. At times, you were given new life in an adult body. Sometimes you lived longer and at other times died earlier."

Sam was so overwhelmed that his only reply sounded really stupid, even to himself. He said, "All those lives and I finished up as a retired construction worker? Wow." Mr. White laughed at this, breaking the tension.

"We have sat here many times over this time period, talking as we are now, Sam. You have had many names through the ages but I think I like 'Sam' the best; it rolls off the tongue easily and seems to suit your personality. Are you ready to go on?" Mr. White asked.

"Go for it," Sam replied.

"It was shortly after your first birth that one of our Atlantis Galaxy Ships landed in the middle of your Atlantic Ocean. "I have often wondered if this was the reason behind its naming in 450 AD. Anyway, you were born in 1589 BC and died the first time in 1525 BC, at the age of sixty-four. You were brought back here and chose to be reborn. You were! Your name at birth was Moses!"

Jumping up, Sam almost shouted. "This is too much! You're nuts! You're trying to tell me that I was Moses, the guy who parted the sea and saved the Israelites?" Sam's mind was going into shutdown.

Mr. White could sense this and he shouted loudly, "Sam, it is only a name and the deeds allotted to it are greatly exaggerated!"

Turning to face Mr. White, Sam stopped and slowly sank back down into his chair. "I have read the Bible and seen the movies of Moses; I know what he did," Sam said.

"Yes, you know the stories," Mr. White answered, "but you have to remember, Sam, they were written by men, written hundreds of years after the facts. You also know writers are prone to exaggeration and making up what makes sense to them to fill in the gaps."

"So you're telling me the Bible is wrong?"

"No, I am telling you time has a way of changing and twisting the truth, records are influenced by the perspectives of their writers."

"Tell me then, what is the truth of Moses—or, should I say, me?"

"You were born an Egyptian, son of the pharaoh, the youngest of two. Your brother was six years older and was well on his way, mentally, to becoming the next pharaoh. He was strong of mind and will and his feelings never got in the way of his path. He could be so cruel at times, never shedding a tear for those he trampled on; he was going to be the next pharaoh. You, on the other hand, were softer, gentler. You always questioned restricting others' thoughts and feelings and rights.

"You always made time to listen to others and make choices based on the idea that only the best for all concerned was the correct choice. You were unselfish, not at all like your brother. This demeanour, which you walked with like a shield, caught the eye of the pharaoh, your father. He knew the next pharaoh should have your traits, not his first son's. He started to favour you. Your brother took notice. He treated the slaves and workers even worse, thinking this would bring favour in his father's eyes.

"Not long after your fifteenth birthday, at the height of his hatred for you, your brother decided you must disappear if he was ever to become pharaoh. He got together with several of the cruellest of his bodyguards and they hatched a plan to take you many days into the desert and leave you to die. The guards were to be handsomely rewarded for this task. Upon their return, your brother had them killed by others in his employ, in this way insuring your father would never find out."

"So, what happened to me then?" Sam asked, much calmer now and interested in the story.

"You died in the desert three days later. Your aura was brought to Atlantica and you were told all about your aura and the way things were done, just as you are being told now. You decided to be sent back at the same age with all your past memories intact. I was not sure if this was the correct choice at the time but bent to your decision. You were placed back in the desert not far from a small town.

"You took up residence in this town while you sorted out what had happened to you. The people of the town were simple people just trying to survive: farmers and herders. They had dreams of freedom from the pharaoh's rule and his taxes. They believed someone would show them the path to freedom; they believed their God would send them this person.

"Weeks, months, and years passed; you were happy to be with people who cared about each other and cared about you. You got a companion and spent many happy times with her and your children. About forty years later, when you were fifty-five years old, you decided to make a trip to see your brother and ask him why he had brought you to the desert. You travelled back home, and took your eldest son, Joshua, with you. When you arrived, your brother was so caught off guard by your visit that he allowed you and your son entrance into his chambers.

"It was here you learned all about your only brother's fears, his hatred, and his betrayal of you. You told him all you wanted were answers, never the throne. You learned your brother had never changed, and had even gotten worse in his cruelty to others. He told you that as long as you left for good he would spare your life. What you did not realize at the time was that your visit had not gone unseen by the masses. This is probably where the rumours about you doing something to get back at your brother began, hence the story of the Plagues.

"Sam, you had no idea at the time that the Abyssinian lakes far to the south were flooding from storms and sending red silt into the river, turning it red all the way to the mouth of the Nile and killing the fish. Or of the fact that crops were dying from this. The locusts were at the peak of their growth and numbers and were in search of more food. I suppose a lot of history is in the timing.

"After learning all you could, you left and headed home to your family. It was your eldest son, Joshua, who stayed, mesmerized by the big city and all its wonders. Years later, Joshua would start the uprising that freed the slaves of Egypt; he was the one to lead them to a new land far away."

Gathering his thoughts, Sam told Mr. White his story was so fantastic it was beyond comprehension—but yet believable. After all, he was here in Atlantica; why would he not believe that this story was the truth? "Let me put all this into perspective in my mind," Sam said. Mr. White just nodded, saying nothing. Sam went on to say, "So, I was born as Moses just before the Atlantis ship came to Earth? Why did the ship even come?"

Mr. White replied, "The ship was brought as a base of operations. This is the same type of ship that originally brought humans to your planet hundreds of thousands of years earlier."

"What are you saying?" Sam asked. "Man did not originate from Earth; we came from elsewhere?"

"That is correct, Sam. We seeded Earth from other more populated planets. Have you not noticed, man is the only species on earth who does not have a natural predator to help in the control of it's numbers. Mans only enemy is himself."

"Why would you seed Earth?" Sam asked.

"Let's go back in our conversations a little," Mr. White said. "Sam, have you, in your lifetime on Earth, ever seen a ghost or heard of others proving they had seen people who had passed away?"

"I remember being afraid of ghosts as a boy and believing that people came back to see their families, but no, I have never seen one or heard factual evidence of others seeing them either."

"The reason no one has seen a ghost is because there is no such thing. When people die, all that remains, for a short period only, are their auras. At the beginning of this process, we utilized the Atlantis ship to store and revitalize peoples' auras. Once the process was completed, these people were given back a living form or were sent to be reborn. If their choice was to be reborn, they were sent into the wombs of young married women, to help population growth. All previous memories were extracted. If they chose a new cloned body with their memories intact, they were given only the option of being sent to another planet in another galaxy. As I said earlier," Mr. White stated, "You were given the rare choice to return fully intact. No one had seen you die and it would have been possible for you to have survived the desert. We—I mean myself and the other Mr. Whites—were curious to see your reactions."

"Why seed Earth?" Sam asked.

"Right," Mr. White replied. "We seeded Earth with humans because there was no intelligent life there; its native creatures survived on instinct only. Man or some other form of intelligence would not have evolved there for hundreds of millions of years." Sam sat forward and told Mr. White about the centuries-old argument of evolution versus creation.

Mr. White, replied quickly. "We have run into this argument on thousands of planets. It happens whenever man has the intelligence to understand science and a form of religion. Man has always had the soul of a poet and the vision of an artist. It seems he cannot exist in a world where there is only one ideal. Evidence of this appears in the ideas of good and evil, sad and happy, right and wrong, and hundreds more. Man has never found contentment; he thrives on inner conflict."

Sam looked at Mr. White and told him he was starting to sound like a philosopher, smiling as he spoke.

Mr. White continued. "But, to answer your question more directly, Sam, this is our purpose. In this universe there are over one hundred thousand, thousand galaxies, with an average of forty million Earth-like planets in each one. Our Charter, if you will, is to spread man throughout the universe. The purpose of this endeavour is beyond even our knowledge."

Sam found these numbers far beyond anything he could imagine. His mind shut them out immediately. Sam's next question was how he had travelled to this galaxy in only two and a half months. Mr. White made a stretching motion with his arms, clenching his fists; he then relaxed them and sat back. "Very simply, Sam, picture the wiring in your house. One wire comes out of the breaker panel and snakes its way through the wall to the first plug-in. From there it continues on to the next and the next. The galaxies are wired in a similar manner, from a central point branching out to other points. In this instance, Atlantica is the breaker box and the wires are travel conduits, with a black hole on each end near the centre of each galaxy.

"Hold on," Sam said. "Black holes suck in and crush anything close to them; this has always been my understanding."

Mr. White smiled. "Yes, we know this is your peoples' belief." He went on, "We are very happy you believe the danger to you is too great to explore further than speculation. Knowledge of our existence is thus prevented two-fold. Let me explain. First, it will be thousands of years before your people have the capability to travel around your own galaxy. The question of going anywhere near the centre, with a black hole there, is not even a consideration.

"Furthermore, each seeded planet houses a device that gathers and contains the auras of all those people dying, keeping them intact till a ship is sent through the black hole to the centre of the galaxy (which only takes micro-seconds). Travelling from the centre to your world is what takes the most time. Your galaxy takes us two months and a bit to traverse; some take years because of their relative size. Our ships are invisible to any of your technologies, so retrieving the auras does not create a hazard for us. Would you like to get up and take a walk around for a few minutes?" Mr. White asked Sam.

"No, I am okay," was the reply. "I am just trying to absorb everything."

Mr. White watched as Sam leaned back in his chair and closed his eyes. He understood what Sam was doing. Once Sam arranged all the information given to him and was able to organize it logically, he reopened his eyes, smiling at Mr. White and saying, "Okay, I am ready to go on. Now for the big question. Why me?"

"Because, Sam, you are one of us! Hold on, let me explain, please."

All Sam's mind could come up with was, What?!

"After you died the first time and were brought back here, all the Mr. Whites received a new command from our makers. We were instructed to add a few extra coloured rings to your aura. When activated, the added rings would give you extra abilities. You could absorb and retain more information than any normal human has a brain capacity to hold. All we were told is that the added storage ability would be used at some future time and that we, the Mr. Whites, would be told when the time came. Now, 3600 years later, this new instruction was enacted when your physical form died."

Sam piped in, "Why was this ability enhanced and what for?"

"I am not finished yet, Sam. Please be patient with me. What I have been doing, telling you about your past, is getting your mind ready to accept and adapt to new information. When you go through the next process, loads of old information will be flooded into your system. We have stored all your previous memories from all your lives here on Atlantica. We will be in control of just how much and at what speed these memories will be given back to you. You can be assured that your new capacity will not be exceeded. The only slowdown is how fast you can accept and organize all this informa- tion. I will tell you right now that we have never done this process with another human. If your brain starts to be overwhelmed, we will have to add some internal micro-circuits to help your system adapt. No, you will not 'become a robot,' as you would say. Think of these circuits as a device, such as a pacemaker, implanted to make sure your heart beats regularly. These new devices are smaller than one of your regular cells. They are undetectable by yourself or any of Earth's scanning technologies."

"Okay, whoa, let me get this straight. A process is about to begin where I will be given so much information that my system may over- load. So, chips or whatever may be installed to make sure I can get all the information and survive? Is this correct?" Sam asked. "Just what information am I going to receive and why?"

"At this time, Sam, I am able to tell you that you will get back each and every memory of every life you have ever had: all one hundred and twenty-seven of them. This is so you will have a one-hundred- percent living history of all the important events and timelines in man's history inside you; you lived through them. The good, the bad, all that has gotten mankind on Earth to where it is today. It is only after you receive all these memories from the past that the scope of the project ahead will be conveyed to you by my superiors. They will give you even more information. This information will give you the ability to make our upcoming project a reality. I do not even know this new information; my superiors will tell you only."

Chapter 4
Oh My

After tossing and turning for most of the night, again, Donna got up and made a fresh pot of coffee. She had been counting the days, weeks, and now months since Sam had been gone from her life. She and Nathan had gotten together for supper on several occasions, but the conversations always came back around to Sam. Donna was slowly starting to get annoyed with Nathan. Nathan missed his friend; he had good intentions and a kind heart but never realized how these conversations allowed Donna to become more and more depressed over the loss of Sam.

Just after Sam passed, Doctor Harvey had prescribed anti-depressants for her, to help take the edge off her loss. The pills made her feel anxious all the time, so she flushed them down the toilet after only a few.

From day one after Sam was put to rest, Donna told herself she had to go on; life just did that! She tried as hard as she could to eat properly with healthy foods and get in lots of walking out in the fresh air and sunshine. On many of her strolls, she sat on a bench and watched kids playing in the park. Watching the children, she imagined sometimes what Her and Sam's kids would have looked like and how old they would now be. She even envisioned grandkids.

Donna kept herself busy, even taking on a new hobby: knitting! As she got better at transforming strings of wool into scarves, mittens, and sweaters, she was able to pay less and less attention to the process of knitting, which allowed her mind to wander off in Sam's direction.

At one point, she even believed getting a puppy might help her moods. Realizing that she lived in a condo that did not allow pets and that she did not want to move again, she let this idea slip away.

Donna realized she would never want a new relationship with any man. She was seventy years old, way too old to put up with a new man's aggravating habits. She'd had a lifetime of trying to straighten out Sam's. She giggled and even smiled, thinking to herself, I almost had him trained; boy, was that work! My dearest Sam, I know you loved me with all your heart; you showed me so. The little things you did each and every day of our lives together...

She decided to call Doctor Harvey again and maybe get some sleeping pills to help her at night. After taking these pills for several days, she awoke late one morning, wondering if this was the way she wanted to start each new day, sleepy and drugged all the time. Her pain had not subsided and she could see no end to her suffering. Maybe, she thought, Sam would be there when she passed away. These thoughts started to take on a life of their own.

Donna believed strongly that no one should take his or her own life. Her church had instilled this belief in her over a lifetime. The battle inside lasted for several weeks. At one point, Donna prayed to God, letting him know that she might take her own life and asking for his forgiveness. Over time, the distinction between desire and obsession became a very thin line. It was not long before she decided to cross it. She had been inconsolable since the loss of Sam, and sheer loneliness made the decision so much easier for her.

Late one night, after making sure the condo was spotless—dishes all done and put away, all the lights off and the door locked—she retired to her bedroom with a large glass of water and two prescriptions of her sleeping pills. Putting the glass and pills on her nightstand, Donna got into her prettiest night gown, brushed her hair, and put the brush back down on the dresser. Standing up and moving over to the bed, she lifted the covers and got in. Sitting up on her side of the bed, covers at her waist, she reached over and took both bottles of pills, dumping their contents on her lap. "Please forgive me for what I am about to do," she said, looking toward the ceiling.

At this point, her mind was already made up. She was convinced that Sam would be waiting for her on the other side. This, to her, was now a guarantee, not just an idea in her mind. Taking the glass of water in her right hand and running her fingers through the pile of pills, she grabbed a small handful and raised it to her mouth. Donna decided to chew the pills into a paste and chase it down her throat with the water; it would go down easier, she reasoned. The pills tasted so bitter. Much better, though, after a swallow of the water. After about two minutes of chewing and swallowing there were no more on her lap. She took one last swig of water and sloshed it around her mouth to get rid of the taste, then swallowed.

Donna put the glass down alongside the empty pill bottles and lids on the bed. The pills were already taking effect in her system. She slowly slid down, pulled the covers up over her chest, brought her hands together above the covers, and entwined her fingers over her mid-section. As far as she was concerned, everything was right with the world and she would now have a good night's sleep. Donna closed her eyes and let herself begin to slip away. She felt at peace with her decision.

•   •   •

Nathan realized he overstepped his boundaries at times, speaking of Sam so much in front of Donna, but he was unaware of just how much this affected Donna, or of the decisions she might make. He was also unaware of just how good she was at concealing her depression. He tried to stay away and let her find her own way, but it was not easy. He and Claire had been friends with Sam and Donna for almost fifty years now. They had never really been separated for more than a few weeks, with holidays and private times for each couple only now and again.

Nathan and Claire alone were privy to the fact that they had known Sam for much, much longer. They had both been sent to

Earth to watch Sam's back by his Mr. White. Their job entailed watching Sam as he grew up and reporting back on how his awareness and ideals grew in this lifetime. They had been watching his growth for many lifetimes. Sam had had some bad experiences in past lifetimes. Some had been through no fault of his own and some he had caused. Nathan was aware that Sam seemed to try harder and harder to better himself morally with each new life.

Of course, Sam was unaware of the changes he was making in this area each time he came back. His memories of past lives were erased with each new life. Sam just seemed to genetically make the changes himself, as if he wanted to make himself a better person. Nathan and Claire had watched him grow from a boy several times, always at a distance, never attracting attention to themselves. They were aware that their spying on Sam could be misconstrued, so they were very careful. The last report sent back to Atlantica let them know, Sam was now ready for what lay ahead.

A few days after Donna ended her life was the day Nathan was invited for their weekly supper at her place. He arrived at five p.m. sharp and rapped gently on Donna's door. He waited quietly for her to open the door. There was no answer. After a few seconds he rapped harder. Still no answer. She never forgot a dinner date with him. A feeling of unease gripped him and he proceeded to try the door knob; the door was locked.

It was only then that his sense of smell picked up a very faint odour. He knew exactly what that smell was and ran back down the hall to his condo and called 911. He gave the emergency service his name and address, mentioned the smell, and asked them to come quickly. Within minutes, an ambulance arrived, along with the police. As the elevator doors opened, Nathan could see the condo super, keys in hand, exit with the police. They moved straight to Donna's door. The super unlocked the door and was thanked by the officer and told that he would take it from here. The super turned and left. Curiosity showed in his face. When the officer swung the door open, the smell of death drifted out in waves.

All present walked in and headed toward the bedroom, where the smell was coming from. There lay Donna, empty pill bottles beside her on the bed. Her skin had changed colour by this time. Nathan needed to see no more; he returned to his condo and closed the door behind him. Tears running down his cheeks, he mumbled, "Why, Donna? Why? Why did you not talk to me first?" Slumping down to the floor, sobbing like a baby, he hugged himself. After several minutes he started to regain some of his composure and stood up. Getting a Kleenex, he wiped his eyes and blew his nose. His first thought now was how happy he was that Donna's aura had been tagged a long time ago, in case of her death. Her aura would be separated from the others in the satellite. His second thought was, "I guess we can all begin now!" A message of this news was relayed to Atlantica.

●   ●   ●

Mr. White spoke to Sam. "At this point, I would like to remind you that you still have a choice. You can be transformed and go on to your new life and leave all this behind. Or you can choose, even though you have no information at this point to make an informed decision, to join us here in making the universe a better place for all of mankind. It all comes down to trust, on your part, that our intentions are for the good of man and not for some other selfish need on our part. I know just how unfair this all sounds. We will respect your wishes, no matter the cost." Just then, Mr. White's com system activated internally. "If you will excuse me for a second, Sam, I need to take a private message," he said. Not waiting for a reply, he leaned back in his chair and closed his eyes.

"Sorry for disturbing you, sir. We just received a message from Earth that Sam's wife, Donna, has passed on. Her aura has already been collected and is on its way back here, accompanied by Nathan."

"This is sad news, as any loss of life is unacceptable," Mr. White replied. "Thank you for this information and for moving quickly on the process of getting her here as soon as possible. Please send my thanks and condolences to Nathan. Mr. White out."

While Mr. White was busy with his message, Sam thought about all the information he had and found himself very comfortable with his gut feeling that Atlantica had no ulterior motives beyond good for him and Earth. The only concern he had was about his role in all this commotion—especially in the mysterious project that Mr. White had mentioned. To say I do not feel a huge amount of excitement about all I have heard and seen thus far—let alone about what the future may hold—would be a huge understatement, Sam thought.

Opening his eyes again, Mr. White said, "Okay, then, before we go on now, I would like you to make the choice to either return back to Earth to be reborn or move on to a new life here."

"Well," Sam started to reply, "You are correct; a lot of information is missing for a proper decision. But, luckily for you, I have a huge amount of curiosity about everything now happening and what is about to happen." Smiling, Sam added, "There is also the fact that I am retired and dead, so I have a lot of free time on my hands." They had a gentle laugh at Sam's last comment. He went on, "Yes, there is trust here. I would love to stay and become a part of this place and your project."

"This is wonderful news, Sam. I am very pleased you have decided to become part of the team here. We will begin the process of giving you a new body in the morning."

"Just one thing," Sam said. "Can I get my old body back, but maybe take off about forty years?"

"Yes, we can do that, Sam. We would be happy to give you the body of a thirty-three-year-old." Mr. White kept his grin hidden from Sam. He was glad of Sam's decision to get his old body back, as this would make the upcoming process easier.

Sam spent most of the evening wandering around inside the room, looking out at the sky and the flying ships going to and fro, up and down. He could feel excitement about the future and getting his new body tomorrow slowly building up inside. It was hard for him to imagine how he felt at such ease now; he had lost so much over the last several months: Donna, Nathan, his other friends, Earth, his body... On the other hand, he had also gained so much. Mr. White, Atlantica—he had proven to himself that there was an afterlife and that there was life in space. His only wish was to have someone to share these revelations with.

Mr. White spent the evening going over reports, speaking to several groups and approving or denying their requests and making small changes here and there within the reports.

Nathan sat alone with the container holding Donna's aura. He watched the stars in each galaxy flash by his window on the way home. He would be so happy to be back at Sam's side again, joined by Donna.

Chapter 5
Transitions

Sam awoke early and headed over to the lounge room, as he called it in his mind. Walking over to one of the windows, he watched as the new day's sun started to rise, covering the city with what felt like a gentle warmth. A voice came from behind him, and with a slight start Sam's thoughts returned to the room. "Good morning, Sam, are you ready to get started?"

Turning to face the voice, Sam said, "And a good morning to you also, Mr. White. Yes, I am."

"Please come with me, then." Mr. White turned and headed to the small raised floor panel on the side of the room. "Step on with me, Sam." Sam got on the pad beside his mentor.

As if by magic—Sam giggled; he was sure this was not the last time he would use that word around here— the pad glowed brightly and a thin wall of light came down from the ceiling and up from the floor, joining together at about waist height. This thin barrier surrounded them. Sam felt like it was also keeping him from moving around.

Suddenly it got very bright, forcing Sam to close his eyes. A few seconds later he could feel the light fade. He opened his eyes and the light shield around them opened in the centre and retreated into the ceiling and floor again. He now found himself and Mr. White standing on a pad in another room, much smaller than the last. Amazing, he thought.

As Sam looked around, he saw several mechanical and electronic machines and consoles around the room. In the centre was what looked like a huge transparent bathtub. There were hundreds of coloured wires and tubes, attached to both sides of a transparent lid which hung suspended by a single large metal tube about five feet above the tub. Mr. White moved first. He walked directly over to the tub and gestured for Sam to follow. Stopping just in front of the tub, Sam saw it was empty, with two drain holes in the bottom and a third opening on the left-side wall, just above the bottom. People wearing light blue robes that went from neck to floor stood at several of the consoles around the room. On their heads they had what looked like everyday headphones with microphones. The room looked so sterile.

There were no visible doors leading out of this room. Looking up, Sam saw several large windows about ten feet up. There were at least a few dozen people, all dressed differently, sitting on benches. They seemed to be speaking very animatedly amongst themselves, though Sam was not able to hear any of their voices.

"Sam, we are now in the revitalization lab, where you will get your new body," Mr. White said. "I cannot stay, but the technicians will explain the process and take good care of you from here." He turned back and walked toward the pad, then got on. The same procedure happened and he was gone.

Looking back at one of the techs, Sam said, "Well, here I am. What will happen next?"

The tech said, "Welcome to our lab, Sam. You will be getting in the tub, as you would call it, lying down, then the lid will be closed and a thick lime-green fluid will be slowly pumped in, submersing you."

Sam quickly protested, "But I will drown!"

The technician smiled, looked around at her colleagues, then back to Sam. "Sorry if your comment looked like it amused me. Let me explain. You are dead, Sam. You may feel like you're breathing, since you have consciousness and awareness, but all that exists at this time is your aura; you are not breathing. Granted, there will be a few seconds when you are immersed that you will feel like holding your breath and panic slightly, but this will pass quickly. Within seconds of being covered with fluid, you will become unconscious. It is this liquid that will generate your new body. Telling you the chemical composition or how all the console's wires and tubes work, or the type of energy used and how everything is combined to make your new body come to life, would take years and you would still be asking questions. You will have to trust us and let us do our tasks, as we have been doing for millennia. You will wake up in your room approximately thirty-six hours from now. All will be well, Sam." The tech placed her hand on Sam's shoulder. "This same question about drowning comes up in this room pretty much every time."

Giving in to trust, Sam stepped into the tub and laid down. The lid slowly came down and he could hear a locking sound. After only a brief moment, the liquid started to be pumped into his chamber. He was only slightly startled. Sam could feel a slight pressure on his aura as the fluid came in contact with it. Just as the tech said, he felt a temporary panic at drowning, but only for a second. At least it's warm, he thought. He became aware that he was drowsy and was being put under.

In the meantime, Mr. White proceeded to reactivate all the alcoves in Sam's room, and the Transfer Pad. Sam would be given a level-one transfer capability for the next week. When he awoke, he would be told about his new access on Atlantica.

Looking out his window, Nathan's com activated and he was told that their ship had only one more galaxy to traverse before the home stretch. They must have been using the ULSHD (Ultra-Light-Speed Hyper-Drive) for the passage through the galaxies to be this close to Atlantica already; only two weeks had passed. Normal speed within a galaxy was only just above light speed: Traverse Light Speed 1.2 (TLS1.2). "Close" being relative, he thought. They were still three-and-a-half million light years away.

Mr. White was informed that all forty-one of the Atlantis Galaxy Class ships required were now sitting in orbit above Atlantica. The ships were being loaded with all the essentials and the personnel required for the upcoming project. Ground factories and cargo ships were working at a feverish pace around the clock. Only twelve times in history had such an armada been required, and all for the same reason. It was never easy for Mr. White to justify to himself what they were about to do. He let these thoughts get pushed to the back of his mind, telling himself that he was too busy getting things ready to be distracted about this mission, the thirteenth one.

•   •   •

Thirty-seven hours and ten minutes later, Sam turned over to his right side in his bed and opened his eyes. Something feels different, he thought. Suddenly, he sat up. Moving his legs over and off the bed, he threw the covers back and placed his feet on the floor. He could now see his legs, arms, feet, and toes. He wiggled his toes on the floor and turned his hands and fingers over and over in front of himself. He was flesh and bone again! He stood up, jumped up and down, and turned around in circles a few times, looking at himself and all his body parts. "Amazing!" he shouted. Tears started to stream down his cheeks as he sat down again on the bed. Reaching up and wiping his cheeks, he put his hands in front of his eyes and saw actual tears wetting his fingers. He licked at the tears and the taste of saltiness was so overwhelming he cried even more. "I am back," Sam whispered.

Just then the door buzzer sounded. Sam said, "Come in." The door vanished and there stood Mr. White.

"You may want to put some clothes on, Sam," Mr. White stated.

It was only then that Sam noticed he was buck-naked. His cheeks turning an instant crimson, Sam looked about the room. He saw his blanket, grabbed for it, and proceeded to wrap it around his mid-section. Looking around again, Sam said, "I guess I will need some to put on; I don't see any here."

Mr. White said, "Okay, lesson number one, Sam." Pointing around the room, he said, "All the alcoves in your room have now been activated. You will have access to all your basic needs here in this room."

Sam was puzzled. He looked at Mr. White and asked, "How?"

Moving over to the first alcove, one of the larger ones, Mr. White said, "All you have to do is press this large button on the top of each alcove and it will activate and light up." Sam walked over and pressed the button. The alcove lit up with a gentle bluish glow.

"Please state type of clothing requested!" A soft female voice came from somewhere in the room. Sam could see no speakers.

"I would like some jeans, a T-shirt, underwear, and a pair of sandals, please," Sam said. As if by some kind of magic, in Sam's eyes, everything he asked for materialized instantly inside the alcove. Jeans on the bottom, T-shirt on top, and underwear and sandals on top of it, all neatly folded. "Wow," was all Sam could say. He reached into the alcove and picked up the pile, then went over and placed it on his bed. He proceeded silently to get dressed.

"As you can see, Sam, everything fits you perfectly, as all your stats were entered into the computer while you were revitalized," Mr. White said.

"I was just going to ask you that question!" Sam exclaimed.

"Before we go on to the other alcoves, let me add that you will return your dirty clothes to this same alcove. After placing your dirty clothes inside, you will press this button here." Mr. White pointed to the next button down. "When you press the button, your dirty clothing will be removed and recycled for other uses. You order new clothing as needed. Basically," Mr. White said, "All the alcoves here and everywhere else on Atlantica respond in the same way." Going through each alcove, Sam discovered he could get clothing, food, liquids, and tools from the different-sized openings. The size dictated what was produced from each one.

Mr. White said, "Don't worry, Sam, if you have one of your hands inside the alcove and you press the second button with the other hand, it will not activate till you remove your hand." Mr. White went on, "As far as food and liquids, you can order anything your heart desires. Every known recipe has been stored inside. If you want items made to your specific tastes, just let the computer know your choices and these will be stored in memory under your identity. Now, as far as this Transport Pad, you have only been given level-one clearance."

Sam asked, "What is, level one clearance and how many levels are there?"

"Level one allows you to Transport anywhere inside this building and also allows you to go to our Central Park. There are three levels of clearance; you will have all three when your rehab is completed in about two weeks." Mr. White added, "Most people never have above a level-two clearance. I will explain all this later. For today, I would like you to familiarize yourself with the alcoves and maybe go to the park. Take some time to relax and clear some of the cobwebs from your head." Mr. White excused himself and left Sam's room.

"All dressed up and no place to go," Sam said out loud to himself, with a big grin on his face. Getting up and moving over to one of the alcoves on the wall, he pressed the top button. It activated and the voice said, "Hello, Sam, how may I assist you?"

Sam said, "I would like a nice hot cup of black coffee, please."

"I am sorry, Sam. You must ask the smaller alcove for liquids. This one is for meals only." The light went out on this alcove. Sam moved his finger down to the smaller alcove and proceeded to get his coffee. Taking it and sitting at his small table, he took his first sip. Sam smiled; it was so nice to feel the hot liquid flow down his throat. His whole body relaxed at the warmth.

"Perfect," he said aloud, "Just like the coffee Donna made." Donna! Her face flooded his mind again. Tears came to his eyes. "I am sorry, sweetheart, I have been so overwhelmed lately I let your memory slide a bit."

Finishing his coffee, Sam stood up and returned the cup to the alcove, sending it off to recycling. Walking across the room, he stepped on the pad. It lit up and the voice asked how she could assist him. Sam said, "I would like to go to Central Park, please!" and closed his eyes, remembering the brightness last time.

Upon opening them a few seconds later, he saw that he was standing on a pad in what looked like a forest. The trees stood very tall. Their trunks were massive, perhaps fifty to sixty feet around their bases. They were separated by about a couple hundred feet. The floor of the forest was covered in a layer of freshly trimmed grass with flower gardens and shrubs of different varieties. Sam did not recognize any of them from Earth.

As far as the eye could see, there were natural ponds and gaze-boes of all styles. There were sitting areas with tables and a small wall with alcoves like those in his room. From his vantage point, he could see a narrow slow-moving river flowing through this part of the forest. The banks of this river seemed to be almost nonexistent; the grass went right up to the edge. Sunlight filtered through the branches and leaves high above. Sam could see, by his estimation, several thousand people within his view. Some were in groups of four to six, many were paired, and others were lying on the grass on blankets having picnics, laughing and chatting together. There were also people sitting inside many of the gazebos, having drinks and food.

It looked funny to Sam; he saw no children or pets running around. Around him and in the distance he saw small colourful birds flitter-ing around, some heading for the upper canopy while others chirped and flew around and landed here and there below. There was just a hint of a breeze, which seemed to carry with it the fragrance of the flowers. There was a real sense of tranquility here. Sam loved it.

Seeing others eat caused his stomach to growl slightly. Sam walked over to the closest gazebo and asked for an iced tea and some fries covered in gravy. The food materialized, napkin and fork included, and he picked it all up and sat at a table. It almost seemed to him that everything was back to normal and he was sitting in a park at home on Earth. It was nice to have this feeling again. Putting his left elbow on the table, he reached for his first fry without the fork and bit off half of it. The flavour of the food was astonishing. Sam's plate lasted what seemed like seconds. The more he ate, the hungrier he was, then they were gone. He picked up his iced tea and washed the rest down. With a small burp, he rubbed his belly, feeling satisfied now. Getting up, he placed his empty plate, napkin, glass, and fork in the alcove and activated it. Walking down to a small pond nearby, he knelt down and looked at his own reflection in the water. He looked exactly as he had when he was in his thirties. Sam felt so invigorated and happy.

Just then, another couple, a man and woman, passed close by. "Hello," the man said. "My name is Robert and this is Helen."

"Hello," Helen said. "We are new here and would like to talk to someone else about all this."

Sam smiled, "Join the club, then; so am I!" They laughed together, breaking any tension. Sam said, "Can we walk as we talk? I have only been inside so far, up until an hour ago. I just got my human form back again."

"Sounds good to me," Robert said. Helen nodded. Robert, looking forward as they walked said, "So, Sam, where are you from?" Sam told him he was from Earth, in the Milky Way galaxy, and asked where they were from. Helen said she was from a planet called Hagala, in Bode's Galaxy. Robert was from Naria, a planet in the Cigar Galaxy.

Sam said, "So, we are all a few miles from home then?" Everyone laughed. Sam found out that Helen had been killed in a war on her planet and that Robert had died of natural causes on his. They too had just been revitalized and met here in the park a few hours ago. They informed Sam that most of the people they had talked to briefly were also new arrivals.

The group chatted for the next hour. Sam told them of his world and they told him of theirs. They learned of the subtle differences in each other's worlds and just how much alike they all were. On the scale of evolution, there was maybe only a few hundred years difference. Politics, religion, and technologies varied in most ways. Some were more fanatical and others more advanced, but all had similarities. They all noted that the advancement and technologies here on Atlantica were so far ahead of those on their planets that they might never understand most of them. They knew nothing of Atlantica's religion or politics.

Sam, Robert, and Helen shook hands at the end of their walk and proceeded back their own ways. Sam had a head full of new information from Robert and Helen to combine with his own thoughts. As he walked toward his pad, he came up with several more questions for Mr. White. Stepping on the pad, Sam returned to his room.

Just after he arrived back from the park, the com system in Sam's room came on; Mr. White's voice asked him to please come to the lounge area. Sam proceeded out his door and down the hall, then walked into the lounge. Far over on one side, he saw Mr. White and walked over to sit down across from him. "Hi Sam, how was your visit to the park?" Mr. White asked. Sam told him about his conversation with Robert and Helen and learning that there was not such a void between Earth's people and those on their planets.

Sam asked, "Where is this park I was at? How big is it?" He had seen no buildings around. Mr. White told him the park was right in the middle of Legost, which was what this city was called. As for size, the park consisted of rivers, streams, forests, valleys, and a mountain range, overall about fifteen hundred square miles.

"Sam, can we move on now to more important things?" Mr. White did not sound short or uninterested in what Sam was asking, but he also had a schedule to follow. "The reason I asked you here is so that I can tell you about your next phase of rehabilitation." Sam nodded his head at Mr. White and asked what step that would be. "Sam, have you realized yet that you only have your last life's memory, not those of all your other lives?"

"You're right," Sam said. "I never really thought about it."

"As I told you previously, you will be given all your old memories. Once that happens, you will talk to my superiors. It will be with them that you will learn the reason for your being here and what is required of you. There will be a short adjustment period prior to meeting them, so that your mind has time to get accustomed to all the new data given to you."

"Alright," Sam said. "When do we start this process?"

"Once again, Sam, we will start in the morning. This is when your mind is most uncluttered and susceptible to learning. The entire Memory Ingram insertion will take at least a few weeks. I will tell you, Sam, that none of the memories you will be getting back include any information about Atlantica or all the times you have been here or what you learned during those returns. We must take your process one step at a time.

"As you can see, Sam," Mr. White pointed to the darkening sky outside, "It is getting late now and you should get plenty of rest. I will say good night to you. Sleep well, my friend."

Sam was taken aback slightly at "My friend." He was not sure what Mr. White meant. Were they becoming friends now, or had they been so for a long time? Mr. White never expanded on the comment and Sam let it drop.

Sam awoke the following morning and was taken to another lab somewhere in the city to begin the memory implant.

As the days slowly passed, Sam was given more and more memories. He was given the odd day off here and there so the memory implants could be more readily absorbed and adjusted to. Sam found some of his memories very disturbing and had a much harder time accepting those. He learned very quickly that he had been no angel in some of his lifetimes. As a matter of fact, he became, at certain points, so upset and disgusted with himself he felt like vomiting. Sam learned that in past lives he had been a farmer, plunderer, salesman, lawyer, mortician, thief, murderer, doctor, and politician. He had done every job he had ever heard of at one time or another in the past several thousand years—and some he never knew existed. Several weeks went by quickly.

●

●   ●

While Sam was going through all this, Nathan and Donna had arrived. Waking up and learning about where she was for the first time was very hard for Donna to accept. She had a much harder time than Sam had coming to terms with her situation. Her Mr. White assumed her processing took longer because this was her first time on Atlantica. He informed her that they did not even consider judging the way in which she had died. The matter of how she died was not important— life was. Donna was informed that how people lived their lives and what they took from them was the most important thing. Did they feel they were good people inside? Were they considerate of the lives they were surrounded by? Did they learn from their mistakes and did they respect the rights of others to make their own choices? In all the universe, these were the most important aspects of a life. Wealth, greed, poverty, politics, and religion had no bearing whatsoever on whom a person was inside.

Donna slowly let her anger with herself for committing suicide fall to the wayside. Once the blame was gone, Mr. White found her every bit as open-minded as Sam to accepting her new life on Atlantica. When it was time for her to be rejuvenated, she was given the same choices as Sam; she decided she too would like to stay and help with the project. Donna also chose to have her own body back at a younger age. Her Mr. White pondered this decision, wondering how two people who did not know each existed could make almost identical decisions. Was there more going on here than even his humanity could grasp?

As always, when Nathan returned he filed all his records in the computer core and told his Mr. White that he was going to find a nice place on the coastline to rest. He would relax for a few weeks—maybe even get drunk!

●   ●   ●

Sam awoke from a very deep sleep in his room. He had finished the last of his memory implants yesterday. He felt groggy and ordered up a cup of coffee while his head cleared. Just as Sam drained the last few drops, the doorbell rang. It was Mr. White. Sam invited him in and told him to have a seat.

Mr. White shook his head, "No, thank you." He asked Sam if he would prefer to go to the lounge or the park for their next discussion. Sam chose the park. He got fully dressed and got on the pad with Mr. White. This time, though, he never heard Mr. White issue a destination. They appeared on another pad a few seconds later, standing on a terrace with a high railing and the usual seating area and a kiosk of alcoves. The view was magnificent. Sam could see the opaque moons high in the sky. Looking down and all around, he saw that he and Mr. White were very high, on the top of a hill overlooking lakes, forests, and rivers far below.

Mr. White motioned for Sam to have a seat. Upon sitting, Sam asked how they got to this terrace when he had never heard Mr. White tell the pad where he wanted to go. Mr. White replied, "I used my mind to picture where I wanted to go and the pad computer extrapolated from that image and sent us here. You now have the same ability, Sam. Yes, I know what you are going to say: how can I think of where I want to go if I have never been there before?"

Sam laughed. "Exactly," he said.

"The computer does not need an absolute destination from you to get you somewhere, just a general idea of the place you would like to go. If you think, "hilltop," "terrace," or "view," the computer will combine your words into an idea. Sam," Mr. White continued, "You have been given a level two clearance and can go anywhere in this city. The pad will never get you into danger or let you into areas you are not allowed to access. You can experiment all you wish; travel around and see the sights."

Mr. White asked Sam how he felt with his head full of old memories. Sam replied, "Not really any different, but different. When I think of something now, I get a whole lot of possible ways to resolve the thought. I just have to choose the one I want."

"There you go, Sam! That is how your brain now works; you do not have to see all the memories associated with each question, just the possible answers. Those answers come from your total combined memories as solutions, very fast and efficient. Not bogged down with full memories. In other words," Mr. White said, "no pictures, just answers. Seeing your way through all those lives has allowed you to pick up information, experience, and skills to make yourself a better person.

"The next step is to meet my superiors. They will fill you in on the details of the upcoming project. They will give you more information than even I have. You will see them in two days' time. Travel around and enjoy yourself in the meantime." With that, Mr. White got up and left.

Sam stood up and walked over to the railing. Standing there, he said out loud to no one, "What is going on? Why am I the one going through all these processes? For what reason? I would like some answers, please." There was no reply. He made a mental note to ask Mr. White's superiors this exact question. After several minutes, he turned from the railing and got on the pad.

He thought, "waterfall," "serene," and "chairs." The pad activated and Sam found himself in what, to him, looked like the Garden of Eden. It was so beautiful he stood just staring at the scenery. Right in front of him was a sitting area, with stone slabs and a slab path leading down toward a small lake. At the water's edge, there was a large dock with very comfortable cushioned chairs, a couch, and a large round coffee table made entirely of what looked like glass. There was also a small kiosk over by the side. Colourful flowers of all kinds bloomed on both sides of the path and plants of enormous size in pots hung from poles attached to the dock. These pots overflowed with long leafy foliage and flowers, reaching down to about six inches from the dock surface. All along and around the edge of the lake, trees stood, each with a canopy of tiny pink flowers. The fragrance was amazing.

Looking out, Sam saw a waterfall that dropped at least five times on its way to the lake. Both sides of the waterfall consisted of steep cliffs covered in what looked like ferns. Sam was astounded by the sense of tranquility this scene brought to his soul. He sat down in one of the chairs. It seemed to move slightly; the cushions con-formed to the shape of his torso and became even more comfortable. Without quite realizing what he was doing, he fell asleep.

When Sam awoke the sun had already set, the first thing he noticed was that the flowers on every shrub, basket, and tree were giving off a kind of very soft fluorescent light. The various colors were mesmerizing. Sam found it easy to walk up the path; the light lit the way very well.

Over the next two days, Sam explored the building he was in and some other parts of the city. Very quickly, he learned not to try to see the tops of the buildings he walked by. They were so tall he almost fell backward several times. There also seemed to be no hustle and bustle, as they say on Earth. Everyone—some with bags but most without—walked, without haste, in and out of the various buildings.

Walking around the corner of one building, he came upon what appeared to be a policeman. The man wore a uniform, a hat, and a badge, but no gun belt or baton. Sam approached him. When he got close enough, the man looked at Sam and said, "Good afternoon, sir. How are you today?"

Sam smiled and returned his greeting. He asked, "Are you a police officer?"

"Yes, I am. I am just making my rounds on this beautiful day. Why do you ask?"

Sam replied, "I saw you standing here from back that way but noticed you did not carry a gun or baton, so I was not sure if you were an officer or not." The officer smiled and told Sam that there was no need for weapons here on Atlantica; there was zero crime. He proceeded to say that he was only here as a memory of security for all the new people walking by; most had police where they came from and it just seemed to feel right to them to see a cop walking a beat. He told Sam to have a good day, then to move along now and stop blocking the sidewalk. He burst into laughter and turned and slowly walked down the street. This encounter made Sam smile as he walked back to the closest pad and went home.

•　　•　　•

During the time Sam wandered around sightseeing, Donna was in another section of his building being given her body back. Her Mr. White followed pretty much the same routine as Sam's had. She was very impressed with the whole process and the attention to detail her Mr. White gave to all her questions and the explanations of the process involved. Donna felt, as Sam did, that she trusted her mentor. When she was asked, by her Mr. White, why she decided to stay here and not go back as a newborn, her answer was very swift. She said it was because she had nothing to go back to. She explained her loss of Sam, her suicide, lack of children, and how even with all the tragedy of late, she was looking for a new adventure and beginning. Donna also knew, being reborn would also be considered a new adventure but she wanted to retain all her memories of Sam and their life together. To her it felt right to have the wisdom of a seventy year old woman in the body of a thirty year old.

Another thing ranking very high on her list of reasons for staying was that she did not have to cook, wash dishes, or even do laundry. Donna and her Mr. White both laughed at that comment.

Several times, Donna's Mr. White and Sam's Mr. White got together privately and discussed how they were still amazed by the strength of the bond between two humans and how long it lasted after they lost each other. The bond humans felt was something just out of their reach; the Mr. Whites wanted to understand it, but even after seeing millions of such events, they were still learning more about the nuances of human relationships.

The Mr. Whites set in motion the plan for Sam and Donna's reunion. This plan was a new instruction they had received from their superiors. For what purpose, they did not know.

Nathan was also given new instructions concerning his friends. He had already been reunited with Claire (for the sixtieth time). They had a beautiful home just on the outskirts of Legost. Sam and Donna had never been aware of the fact that Nathan, Claire, and their kids had all been implants on Earth. This implanting as a growing family unit helped in the illusion presented to Sam and Donna.

Nathan and Claire were known on Atlantica as Providers. They were one of millions of teams sent all over the universe, relaying real-time messages home to let the superiors know what was going on with planets that had been seeded. Nathan and Claire were synthetic humans like the Mr. Whites. Their programming was slightly different, however; they could show more emotion, thus blending in better with the humans.

Nathan and Claire had been told, way back when, that the superiors were aware of future events on Earth. They had been told about the overpopulation issue and knew something needed to be done. Based on the facts coming to them, they knew prevention was going to be necessary soon, within a few hundred years, at most. This time span was a billionth of a second in terms of cosmic time.

●   ●
    ●   ●

The two days flew by for Sam. On the third day, Mr. White entered his room and asked him if he was ready to meet the superiors. Sam told him he was. Mr. White went on to say, "We, meaning all the Mr. Whites here, have never seen our superiors. We only receive instructions on our com systems."

Sam jumped on that. "Are you not even curious about what they look like or who they are?"

"No, we are not. As I said before, we are happy and content with the direction given to us by them." Mr. White continued, asking Sam, "If you were all alone in the desert, dying of thirst, and you came over a sand knoll and found an oasis with water and fruit trees, would you be asking who made this paradise and what they looked like? Or would you run down to it and take your fill?"

Sam thought for a second, then replied, "I would take my fill first, but I would still wonder how and why it was there, in the middle of nowhere."

"Perhaps, Sam, curiosity about the superiors was never programmed into us?" Sam let this answer appease him.

"Okay, then," Sam said. "Where are we going?"

"Not 'we,' Sam, just you! Please get on the pad and think or say, 'Meet superiors.'" Sam stepped on the pad, closed his eyes, and followed Mr. White's instruction.

Opening his eyes, Sam looked about the very large room he was now in. He could see no chairs or benches. The walls on all four sides, including the ceiling high above and the floor, were black. In the middle of the room was a huge glass cube, approximately twenty-five feet square. The cube appeared to balance on just one of its eight corners. It was filled with a cloudy translucent smoke. There seemed to be bright objects deep within this smoke, dancing and swirling about almost like flames in a fireplace. It was impossible for Sam to make out how many objects were inside the cube. He could not identify anything he was seeing inside. The bright objects inside the cube, filtered by the smoke looked to be the only lighting in this room.

Sam stepped off the pad and slowly approached the cube. Within ten feet, he felt chills. Goose bumps rose on his arms and his hair started to stand up. It felt like static electricity. He stopped and backed up a few steps. The static charge dissipated; his goose bumps and the sudden chill he felt slipped away. "Hello! Is anyone here?" Sam whispered. As he stared into the smoke, the bright objects inside started to move around a little faster, as if sensing his presence and question.

"Hello to you also, Sam." A voice filled the room all around him. It was neither loud nor soft. "I and the others here are pleased to have this chance to speak with you."

Sam replied, "I, too, am happy to be here. Can you all tell me who you are, why I am here, and what it is you want from me?"

"Yes, Sam, we can answer all those questions for you and more. This will take time and patience on your part; would you like to sit while we explain?"

Just then, about two feet from where he was standing, an invisible panel in the floor slid open and a comfortable-looking armchair rose to floor level. "Thank you," Sam said. "I think I might just stand for a little while first."

"Very well," the voice spoke. Sam slowly walked around the base of the cube, trying to see inside from different angles.

"We will proceed with the premise that you are not a brilliant astrophysicist or a geophysicist, just a man of normal intellect," the voice said. "We must inform you right from the start, you are never to discuss with anyone what you will learn about us in this room. To do so would forfeit your aura and theirs. So you have a full understanding, both auras would instantly dissipate and never again be cohesive. We included this feature into one of your new rings for our security. If you understand what we said and agree, say 'yes,' and we can move on from here. If not, you have the choice to leave this room and no more will ever be said."

Thinking for only a second, Sam replied, "Yes, I agree to this request."

"So be it," the voice said. "Let us start with the basics then, to help you understand. Sam, on Earth, one of your technologies is the electron microscope."

"Yes, I know what it is and how it is used—to see things one- to two-hundred-thousand times smaller than I can see with my eyes."

"That is correct," said the voice. "If you have seen pictures of the magnification of an object, you have noticed that as magnification increases, structures look more and more complex. Once you reach the maximum magnification of this device, you may be left still wondering how much further you could go till there is nothing to see."

"That is exactly how I felt," Sam stated.

"Have you ever wondered, Sam, about how the way protons and neutrons circle around an atom looks so much like a sun and planets in orbit? Perhaps they could be the same, just on a different scale?"

"I will admit, I never thought of it that way," Sam said.

"What we are trying to get you to see, Sam, is that size does not matter; everything has a purpose. What if you were able to see so far down with your electron microscope that you could see beings walking around on their planets, driving cars and flying planes? Would this blow your mind?"

"More than likely," Sam replied.

"Okay then, let us put this scenario in reverse," the voice stated. "What if you could look all the way past the size of your whole universe and beyond and see that it was just a single cell inside a larger being? How would this affect you?"

"I have no idea," Sam said.

"Let us take this thought one step further," the voice said. "What you would be seeing, looking down one size scale then up the next size scale, would be different dimensions of the same thing. As far as you are concerned, this is who and where we are from: the dimension just above yours, the fourth dimension. We exist in another plane; that is why you cannot see us. There are also beings from your universe using a cube like this in the one below it, communicating with the beings of that dimension."

Sam decided to sit down. His brain was being taxed; he had to think about the scope of all this. He spoke, "What you are saying is that there are whole universes above and below this level and that each of these has a level above and below it? They are called planes of existence? Just how many are there?" Sam asked.

The voice quickly said, "We have no idea, but we can tell you that each one has an effect on the one above and the one below it, and so on and so on."

"Your scientists on Earth are just coming around to envisioning the possibility of other dimensions. They feel there is something missing in the big picture of particles and their interactions with one another. They think that if they can find what is acting on the particles they are aware of, they can solve the mysteries of the universe. They are on the right track. The way you now see us, inside this cube, is our way of getting to this dimension. We cannot leave this cube nor can you enter it."

"Let us expand sideways a bit here," the voice said. "We will start by telling you that all the atoms in your universe are solid matter; they form the building blocks of everything in it. This solid matter makes up all your galaxies, stars, planets, moons, asteroids, and all that is on them. This matter accounts for about fifteen percent of your universe. The other eighty-five percent is made up of dark matter particles; you cannot see or feel their existence. You can think of dark matter particles as the empty space or vacuum between the solid objects that make up your universe. Each molecule of this dark matter only exists for a millisecond before it explodes and creates new dark matter particles. These explosions create energy, so little you cannot even measure their existence. It is from an accumulation of these tiny explosions that Atlantica gets its energy— inexhaustible and more than can ever be used at any given moment.

"Atlantica uses particle collectors to gather and store this energy. This is the sole purpose of one of its moons. The moon is the collector, storage device, and distributer all in one. These collectors are used all over the universe to supply power to the transit conduits, ships, and planets we seed. The collectors are only activated on each of those planets when people are mature and advanced enough to utilize the technologies involved."

Sitting in his chair, Sam listened to all this information and felt it was filling in the gaps in his understanding thus far. The superiors were making it easy for him to understand, speaking at his terminological level. Sam knew they could have talked so far above his level it would have sounded like jibber-jabber to him; he was grateful they had not.

"Are you getting a grasp on the information so far, Sam?" the voice asked.

"Yes, thank you," he replied.

"Now let us look at the human brain," the voice said.

"The human brain? What?" The words jumped out of his mouth. Sam brought his hands up. "Sorry, go ahead," he said.

The voice went on. "Picture the human brain. It controls everything to do with the body's life: breathing, thinking, moving, and the regulation of all the organs. You would not have life without the brain's control. Now picture, if you will, a microscopic blood clot preventing blood flow into just a tiny capillary of one of the veins coming off an artery. Do you know what this is called, Sam?"

"Yes, it is an aneurysm, or stroke."

"If this happens," the voice said, "That tiny insignificant clot can render the entire body useless; the face droops, the left arm and side of the body become numb, and the ability to speak coherently is lost. A stroke can even effect shutdown of major organs and kill the body."

Without being told, Sam had begun to see the picture the voice was painting. He understood that size did not matter; even the smallest thing going wrong could have a rippling effect, like waves on an ocean washing away the shoreline. Speaking up, Sam asked the voice what the brain had to do with him and why he was here.

The voice went on. "What we are trying to say, Sam, is that we are from the brain, if you will, in our dimension. Earth is going to become like a clot in your universe. Its effect on your universe will have effects on ours and the one below yours; these will expand outward over time. We have no idea of the overall end result, only that we have to stop your Earth in its current course."

This last statement was a whopper to Sam, like getting punched in the head by a professional boxer. All he could muster was, "How is Earth going to cause a problem and how could I possibly be able to fix it?"

The voice said, "Here it is, in what you would call a nutshell. The population of your Earth is at around seven and a half billion people. At ten billion, a virus will be released by your planet, killing all life and removing all atmosphere. It would be wiped away forever."

Eyes bulging, mouth opening, all Sam could ask was, "Why?"

"Sam, you have to understand, the earth you live on is a living, breathing organism. Its life depends on feeding, processing, and expelling matter, just like yours. It emits oxygen and nitrogen into its atmosphere from plant life, allowing new life to grow. It consumes waste material and expels it as volcanic rock and carbon monoxide. This cycle is continuous; it never stops until death, just as is the case with your body."

"I understand this process, but why will a virus be released?" Sam asked.

"Sam, you have to understand, all of life exists only because there is a balance. If you tip the scales slightly one way or the other, life will find a way to rebalance them again. Here is one quick example for you, Sam. If you catch a cold virus, you get sick because your immune system was not prepared for the attack. Your body will create white blood cells to fight off the virus. When there are enough of these cells to kill it, your body goes back to normal production. The virus is gone and the balance is restored. If your body, for whatever reason, could not produce these white blood cells, even a common cold could kill.

"Well, Sam, this is what is happening to your Earth. Your population growth, with all its polluting, nuclear waste, and over-consumption, is going to overwhelm the ability of the Earth to rebalance itself. This is where you come in, Sam.

"We have been grooming you for the past thirty-six hundred years, your time, to have the ability to help us resolve this problem before a worst-case scenario can happen. We are not allowed physically into your plane of existence, so you were chosen at random to be the one. By our estimate, there are about one hundred and eighty years, your time, before there is no going back," the voice stated.

"You keep saying, 'my time.' Why?" Sam asked.

The voice answered, "Because, Sam, your time moves at a much faster rate than ours does. By our time, we have a hundred thousand years to solve this. We prefer to be proactive rather than complacent."

Sam was getting scared now. Raising his voice, he asked, "And just how in the hell am I supposed to solve this problem on my own?"

"Please relax, if you can, Sam. We would never think of having you undertake a task of this size alone. A team is being assembled as we speak. Your Mr. White will explain all the details and tell you about the members of your team later. We wanted you here to give you—and only you—the big picture, as you would say. All the other members of your team only know there is a project coming up to help Earth in its transition to becoming a much better place for man to live. Speaking from our hearts, if you will, you are going to be very pleased with the team you will be in charge of. All of the Mr. Whites have been informed of the plans. After all, Sam, it is your Earth and always has been."

"This grooming I have had—what is the reason for that?" Sam asked.

"You were sent back to Earth every time you were rejuvenated; thus, you have a continuation of memories of how mankind got to this point in time. You are the only one with all the real facts because you actually lived through them. There is no guesswork involved on our part. You have seen the rise and fall of entire civilizations, and seen what the causes were. It is this accumulation of memories that will help you navigate a solution for your planet. When a question arises, you will be able to draw on all those memories to give a solid and rounded answer."

"Yes, my Mr. White told me as much," Sam replied. "There is still one big question I have that Mr. White never did give me an answer to, though. Why seed Earth, or any other planet, for that matter? Is man not the one doing all the harm to these planets?" Sam asked.

The voice responded, "You are right; man does have the habit of causing most of the problems on planets. Overall, though, once man learns that he must live in balance with his surroundings, a kind of bond is created. This can be seen in the health of the planet, which seems not to have as many natural catastrophes. The weather is milder and the oceans teem with life. Also, Sam, the seeding of the planets provides extra nourishment, through decay, to the soil of the planet. Even though the material of this nourishment is small in quantity, it also has an effect on the well-being of the planet, just like when the dinosaurs died."

Sam piped in, "So, what you are saying is that the decay of our bodies feeds some need of the planet."

"Yes, Sam, it is like giving an aspirin to stop a headache," the voice said. "As small as the pill is, its effect works wonders.

"All the Mr. Whites and the humans in your universe believe your universe is all there is. You are the only one with the knowledge that there are so many more, above and below. Man is not yet ready to believe he is really so insignificant in the scheme of things. As we come to a close here, let us tell you that one more ring of colour has been added to your aura, for a total of six. This last one will allow you to communicate with us at any time; just say, in your head, 'speak to Cube.'

"Sam, the fate of Earth is being left in your hands. Atlantica will supply what you need. They have taken steps to prepare, based on previous issues of this kind. You now have access to all of Atlantica's knowledge and its technologies, with a level ten clearance. All this will be explained by Mr. White. Now it is time for you to leave us and start moving the project forward."

The cube slowly went dark, the pad light came on, and Sam was all alone. He walked over to the pad and left.

Returning to his room, Sam got food and a drink from the kiosk. He stood facing the empty wall and said, out loud, "Computer on." A large portion of the wall instantly became a screen. Just below it, the wall moved outward toward him and became a desk. A plate in the floor opened and up came a chair for him to sit on. There was no keyboard or mouse. For some reason, he already knew how to do all this and also knew that the computer was controlled by voice command. Sam was surprised by this new ability but yet not really surprised.

Placing his plate of food and glass on the table, he sat down. "Map of Legost, please." A map of the entire city appeared on the screen, showing Central Park right in the middle, with a flashing red beacon showing his location. He was at the central edge of the city just beside the park.

"Please show me all the Mr. Whites." Within a second, the screen filled with thousands of blue dots. "Highlight my Mr. White"; all the blue dots except for one disappeared, leaving Sam to see his Mr. White in the same building as him. Without a second thought, he said, "Mr. White, could you please come to my room when you have a chance?"

Instantly Sam got a response: "I will be there in five minutes, Sam, nice to have you back." With five minutes to kill, Sam looked at different places on the map and even expanded it to a view of the planet. He was a little surprised; if the park was fifteen hundred square miles, then Legost must be about fifty thousand square miles. A number immediately showed on bottom of the screen in small writing: "46,600 square miles."

The door chimed, opened, and in came Mr. White. "Hello Sam, I trust all went well with the superiors?"

"Yes, everything is all good," Sam replied. "They told me you would fill me in on my levels of clearance. I know there are ten levels; I am not sure what each one entails. I am guessing," Sam went on, "if I have level ten, the rest are not so important. Can you please inform me about that one?"

Mr. White told Sam that level ten gave him access to any and all information in Atlantica's computers and allowed him to travel to any place on the planet or the moons around Atlantica. Sam could board any ship on or in orbit around the planet and take charge of any vessel he chose. He could go anywhere in the entire universe. Sam was told he was now the one in charge of Atlantica, including its entire armada and all the Mr. Whites.

They would take direction from him in any matters concerning Atlantica or the project. Sam was told he did not have to worry about the day-to-day operations of Atlantica, as these were all taken care of by the Mr. Whites. This freed up his time up to work on bigger things.

"Wow," Sam said. "How did I go from being an old dead human to getting put in charge of everything?"

"This is at the request of the superiors, and I must say I am in agreement," Mr. White said. "You must remember, Sam, there is no jealousy here. We each perform our duties to the best of our abilities for the good of all; the one does not matter. I suppose you are having a feeling of, 'Just where do I start?'"

Sam said, "I know nothing of Atlantica except what I am learning right now. I was never given knowledge of this place when I got my memory implants."

"There is a reason for this," Mr. White replied. "The superiors wanted someone not predisposed to run Atlantica as it was before; they wanted new direction from someone fresh. This is not to say that Atlantica was run badly before, but just that it needs some new ideas and enthusiasm.

"We, meaning all the Mr. Whites, are behind you and our support will never have to be questioned, Sam. Yes, this is the result of a directive, but we also were given a choice whether or not to accept you. We chose the latter. So now, Sam, let us speak of the project."

Mr. White filled Sam in on the ships in orbit and the preparations underway. Sam was told his team was being assembled and would be ready to sit down with him in just a few weeks. He was told to go ahead and relax; all was progressing well. Sam felt reassured, though he was not yet even sure how to start the project or what tools he would have at his disposal.

•   •   •

Having her body back felt very good to Donna; she had never felt better and even thought she was beautiful again. Donna was once again thirty years old, with all her previous life's memories. She never wanted to give up her memories of Sam and the life they had, though she had never told her Mr. White this part. Looking into the large dressing mirror on the wall of her room, she noticed her long dark brown hair, her tiny waist, muscular thighs and calves, and, oh yes, her smallish but perky breasts. She touched them; they were so firm compared to what they had become in her later years on Earth. She smiled. She was very pleased with this new body. Just after using the kiosk to get clothing and getting dressed, her door chimed and she welcomed her Mr. White.

"Hello Donna, how are you making out with the transition to your new body and life here?"

Donna replied, "I feel wonderful and I think I am going to enjoy my new life here on Atlantica." Mr. White reminded Donna of their previous conversation about her involvement with a project Atlantica was about to start. She told him she remembered and wondered what her role was in it. Mr. White informed her that someone would explain this to her soon.

Mr. White told Donna to go out into the city today and enjoy herself and see some of the sights. Later that evening, he would have a surprise for her. Donna giggled out loud. "Tell me, tell me, what, is the surprise?" she said, gently punching him in the arm. Mr. White smiled. He found women so inquisitive; they always wanted to know what a surprise was but did not really want you to tell them about it. Amazing.

Sam was deep in thought as he sat looking at one screen after the other showing maps, ships, energy converters, weapons, propulsion drives, and other technologies Atlantica possessed. He was trying to get a handle on what he could use for the upcoming project on Earth. Several hours passed without him realizing it and his mind began to turn to mush. "Time for a break," he thought. The screen went blank and turned off. Sam was still amazed, all he had to do was think about something when sitting at the computer and it happened.

He was just getting ready to leave his room after showering, shaving, and getting dressed when his com system came on. It was Mr. White, asking him to come to the lounge so they could speak. Sam acknowledged the request and headed down the hallway.

It was about six p.m. when he walked into the lounge and sat down across from Mr. White. "What's up?" Sam asked.

"I and a few other Mr. Whites got together and have planned something for you, to help you relax. At seven p.m. sharp, get on a pad and say, 'Activate Mr. White one.' Please do not ask why; the reason will become self-explanatory once you arrive."

"Wow!" Sam said. "A mystery! I love it. No problem, I can do that."

"Oh, and by the way, Sam, dress nice!"

"The plot thickens," Sam said with a laugh. "If that's all, I better go now and dress." Sam paused for a second, then held the two middle fingers from each hand in the air to indicate quotation marks. "Nicely," he said sarcastically. Laughing now, he turned and headed out of the lounge.

At seven p.m. sharp, Sam got on the pad in his room, used Mr. White's activation sequence, and found himself in the waterfall area he had visited once before. The sun had just set and all the plant life glowed. Looking down the path toward the lake, he saw someone sitting in one of the chairs, looking out over the lake toward the waterfall. As Sam walked closer, he made out a woman with long brown hair. In one hand, she had a glass of wine; the bucket with the bottle sat on the table in front of her. Beside the bucket he saw an empty glass. When Sam got within six feet of the chairs, the woman turned her head toward him.

Their eyes met and locked. Her glass dropped from her fingers and shattered on the deck. Neither of them saw the small door at the bottom of the kiosk open and a small cleaning-robot device come scurrying out to clean up the spilt champagne and broken glass and then retreat back inside the kiosk.

"Donna?" Sam gasped and fell to his knees, tears of recognition streaming down his cheeks. He started to sob. Donna jumped up, took the two steps to him, and went down on her knees in front of him. She reached out and placed her arms around his neck and hugged him tightly, crying.

"Oh, Sam! Is it really you? Please say it is. I have missed you so much! Please, please, say it is you?" After what seemed like hours, with both of them sobbing and holding each other tightly, Sam winced. In a muffled voice, he said, "You're choking me; I can't breathe," and nudged Donna gently backwards. She released her grip and leaned back, staring into Sam's eyes. She reached up with both hands and tried to wipe away her tears. Sam leaned back, took a deep breath, and wiped his own eyes.

Donna spoke first. "How? Why? What is going on?"

Sam, at loss for words, said, "Who cares? We have each other back." They hugged again.

Just then, a familiar voice behind them loudly said, "Oh Jesus, get a room, you two." Donna looked up and Sam turned around and there were Nathan and Claire walking arm in arm on the walkway toward them. Sam and Donna jumped up and ran toward them. Nathan and Claire opened their arms and welcomed their friends into them. Now they were all crying and speaking at the same time, no one understanding a word anyone else was saying. After several minutes, they pulled apart and laughed with joy before hugging each other again.

The couples went over to the chairs and couch and sat down across from each other. They sat for a minute not saying a word, each in their own way trying to imagine all this. Sam got up, went over to the kiosk, and got three more wine glasses and another bottle of champagne. He sat the glasses and wine down beside the opened bottle, popped the cork off, and filled all the glasses.

Sitting down, Sam took his glass in hand and made a toast to all of them, thanking them for being back in his life again—especially Donna. They all laughed and took a swallow of the wine, then spent the rest of the evening, into the wee hours, catching up. The champagne and food flowed all night. Thanks to the weather-controlling satellites, the sky remained clear and the temperature around seventy-two degrees.

Sam learned of Donna's suicide, but—just like the people of this world—he had a new sense of life being the important thing, not how one died. He told Donna there was no forgiveness required; she was here now and that was all that mattered. Sam and Donna learned that the reason for Claire's death on Earth had been because she had been called back to Atlantica.

Nathan and Claire explained who they really were and what their jobs were here on Atlantica. Sam was slightly taken aback to learn that his best friends were from Atlantica and had been on Earth to report on him and how he was progressing with his humanity—and making a judgment on if he was ready to do the work coming up.

At this point, Donna asked all of them about her involvement in the upcoming project. Nathan spoke first, as Sam was not even sure about that. After all, he had only learned of her existence several hours ago.

"You were rushed back here at the last moment because the superiors believed having a familiar face beside him would help Sam with his talks on Earth and that the two of you, both from Earth, would represent how the people of Earth mostly presented themselves. Kid yourselves not, you two, there will be, I am sure, many decisions you will have to make which will be very hard. Though as a couple you are strong and undivided, this may test your bond and beliefs in each other.

"Remember, we are close to all of mankind on Earth being eliminated. It will be up to us to make sure this does not happen. If it does, we will move on as we always have, knowing we tried our best. There are more things in heaven and earth than the mortality of a single planet's population. There is a greater good to all of this; you just have to believe this is where your strength will come from. Anyway, Donna, I will let Sam fill you in from this point."

Nathan and Claire stood up and hugged Sam and Donna one more time. They told them they should stay and become acquainted again; there was a long road ahead. Nathan and Claire walked up the path to the pad, waved, and were gone.

Sam went on to tell Donna all he was allowed to. How he met the superiors and how they had asked him to help with the project. He told her about the Earth releasing a virus and what the end result would be if they failed. He never mentioned anything about other dimensions or what the superiors looked like, not even about the cube; he was not allowed to.

Sam and Donna spoke about her life after he had died and how amazed she was that there was an afterlife and that Sam was also here. Sam told Donna he was now in charge of Atlantica and how it was up to him and his team to figure out how to get the people of Earth to listen and make changes, changes which would bring harmony between the people and the Earth itself. He told her how the Earth was an actual living organism and needed assistance to get back in balance.

Sam also informed Donna about all the lives he had lived and how the superiors had groomed him for this project. Donna would have to receive some of Sam's memories to bring her up to speed on the way Earth had progressed over the last thirty-six hundred years. Sam told Donna that Atlantica had seeded Earth more than one hundred thousand years ago and why.

By the time they finished talking, the sun was just starting to rise over the horizon. Sam and Donna were both very tired. They got up and walked to the pad, got on, and Sam thought, "Home, please."

A moment later, they got a huge surprise. The pad they stood on now was in a huge home on the shore of a large lake. Both Mr. Whites were there to greet them. One of the Mr. Whites spoke up, saying, "Welcome to the both of you. This is your new home, a gift from the two of us." Sam and Donna looked at each other and smiled. They had the same thought at the same time; they nodded to each other.

Sam spoke up. "Okay, you two are identical and that cannot continue; one of you must make some kind of alteration so we can tell you apart." One of the Mr. Whites closed his eyes and his long white hair turned dark brown, just like Donna's.

"You can now call me Mr. Brown. I am Donna's Mr. White. Sam and Donna both burst out laughing. They thought the change was brilliant. Mr. White and Mr. Brown told them to get some rest in their new home for a few days and that they would be back then to get them up to speed on the preparations. Over those next few days, Sam and Donna spent lots of time hugging, holding, talking, and making love. They became husband and wife again, but with a much clearer picture of how they wished to proceed.

Chapter 6
Let Us Begin

After their brief respite from the rest of the world, Sam and Donna were visited by Mr. White and Mr. Brown and Nathan and Claire. Donna was told that during the journey to Earth she would get the new memory implants from Sam and have time to assimilate them before the work started. They were informed of the forty-one Atlantis Class Ships at their disposal and what each ship carried as far as equipment and personnel. Sam and Donna told the group some of the ideas they had for helping Earth transition from where it was presently. They agreed that most of the ideas sounded good but that contingencies would also have to be thought about, considering the stubbornness of humans.

Sam had decided they would all go in the first ship, to let Earth know of their arrival. The other ships would proceed about two months behind them and wait at a designated spot in the Milky Way for his command to enter Earth's orbit.

With a basic game plan laid out, the group got on pads and arrived at their ship, the Excelsior. Sam and Donna knew from looking at all the specifications just how big and fantastic these ships were. An Atlantis Class ship was twice the size of Manhattan Island: about eighty square miles, with a gross weight of six hundred million tons. The ships were circular in design and stood just over a mile high. There were no photon torpedoes or ray guns. Weapons were limited in space; they served no real purpose.

There were only a few thousand planets in the universe with space travel capabilities. The idea of conquering or going to war with another planet would be dealt with harshly by Atlantica: all space travel and exploration abilities would be taken away and the ships destroyed, sent into the nearest star. Atlantis ships carried five hundred shuttles, each capable of carrying one thousand people and serving various other purposes. Also on board were several hundred fighter-class interceptors. These very rarely saw any action, but their pilots kept up on training. The ships had over five thousand crew members and accommodation for three million guests.

At the time specified by Sam, the ship left the orbit of Atlantica and began its journey. The team had about two and a half months to tweak their plans. Needless to say, the time went by very quickly. The ship arrived in the Milky Way galaxy and came to a stop just one hundred million miles from Earth. Time for their first message to be sent!

●   ●   ●

Sam knew, from each of his lifetimes, that there was a secret society, unseen and unheard-of, operating behind the scenes. No single person ever knew the entire pyramid chart of super major corporations and all their subsidiaries. What the Earth's total business community came down to was about twenty-seven massively huge corporations, hidden by all the paperwork.

These corporations, at the highest level, were run by only nine individuals. There was no one in the entire world they did not have some control over. Presidents, kings, queens, billionaires, and the little folk were used like pawns in a chess game to satisfy their greed and need for power and money. They loved the game, no matter who or what got hurt. As each of the nine individuals grew old and died, a new member was recruited to fill the gap.

This went on for hundreds of years. If the people of the world really knew this was going on, Sam was not sure what effect it would have, except that it would not be good. Each member came from a different country, where they had climbed through the ranks of business and heredity to get where they now were.

Eight of the individuals were men and one was a woman. They all had families and looked just like normal business people. On average, they met once each quarter and divvied up between them the tasks and spoils of their efforts. They all felt they could control the world better than any government. This group of individuals had the training and skills to master the group-think ideal. Meaning that even though they did things separately, their goal was the same: control. Many times, the nine could not agree with each other, so their own written bylaws dictated the outcome of controversial decisions. These bylaws were their Holy Grail.

Each person was in control of different aspects of the world economy. The money they made from their respective corporations allowed them to play the games they did. They were fully aware that money was the key to power and used it to perfection.

These people were individuals but operated as a single global entity. It was like a person working all week at a menial job, then coming home and playing monopoly with a group of friends, except that these were not friends. They seldom communicated with each other outside the boardroom, though they had a similar goal: money.

Sam's first message was sent to these individuals. All nine members had been kept tabs on for some time now. It was up to the Providers on Earth, the Mr. Whites in disguise, to notify them and convince them all to come, by themselves, to a central location in the middle of the Sahara Desert. This task was huge but the enticement they were offered made them respond very quickly. Each member was told new technologies would be given to them. These technologies would make them even richer.

One example the Mr. Whites showed them was a food kiosk like those on Atlantica. This kiosk was the only one on Earth; the Mr. Whites used it to accommodate the special tastes they had acquired over many years. This was exactly the way to the members' hearts. Each one informed the department heads below them that he or she was going on vacation and did not want to be disturbed for any reason. The security personnel were surprised by their requests but relented all the same; this was the boss asking and "no" was not an option. The members were told they would be taken for a meeting with Sam and his team on board a spacecraft.

Sam was notified on the fourth day after his arrival that the nine were ready for transport. Each had a thousand questions for the Providers who brought them there. All they were told after the initial contact was that information would be forthcoming from Sam. For the first time in a very long while, they felt as if they were not in control; it was very unsettling for them, to say the least.

●

●

●

The group of nine stood nervously in the middle of nowhere when suddenly the large vessel, about the size of a city block, materialized just five hundred feet from them. They watched as the ship touched down without a sound and a door about thirty feet from the ground materialized on the side they could see. Next, a ramp made its way to the ground. As it touched the ground, the group was asked to please enter the transport. Walking up to the ramp, each individual stepped on and grabbed for a handrail; they were moving up the ramp. They could see no belt or other device propelling them slowly up; it was almost like they were drifting upwards on their own. "Amazing," each one thought as he or she rode up the ramp.

At the top they were guided into a sitting area mid-ship and asked to have a seat. They were told their trip would not take too long and that they would soon have their questions answered. After sitting, they were provided refreshment and told that they could watch the large screen on the front wall; they would be able to see what the pilot sees as he headed to their destination. As they watched the screen and drank their drinks, talking amongst themselves, their screen showed them lifting straight up, then turning and picking up speed, though they felt no movement whatsoever.

One of the nine asked a question about this movement. He was told there was an inertial dampening system integrated into the vessel to make their ride comfortable and avoid the action of gravitational forces on their bodies. Of course they all thought about how this might work and how they could make money from it. The Mr. Whites on board smirked at each other and at the nine. No end to their greed, they thought, shaking their heads.

The guests saw they were now rising quickly through Earth's atmosphere and heading into the darkness of space. They watched as the moon and some of the other planets flew past them as they headed out of the solar system. They were both stunned and amazed by all this. They knew that no one on Earth had the technology to do what these people were doing. Looking at each other without speaking, the Mr. Whites saw that these people could actually show fear. They smiled.

With the solar system behind, a bright light came into view. Everyone watched the screen as they got closer and closer to what they could now identify as a much larger vessel. Their vessel appeared to slow and the bigger vessel's size seemed to increase. Soon the ship took up the entire screen and still got bigger. They noticed a huge door opening in the surface of the larger ship and knew they were going inside.

They entered the first large room, the airlock, before their ship proceeded into the main hanger bay. Once they were inside, the outer door closed and fresh air, under pressure, replaced the vacuum of space. When the pressure equalized, the main hanger door opened and they continued inside to a landing pad. As they passed the door, the screen went black. The passengers caught only the briefest glimpse of the inside, which was extremely large and cavernous. Within minutes, the lights in their cabin brightened and the door they had come in reappeared. They were politely directed to disembark.

As the nine rode the escalator down to floor level, they tried to grasp just how huge this hanger arrival area was. From what they could see within their lines of vision, there were perhaps hundreds of vessels the same size as the one they had arrived in.

As soon as they reached floor level, an open-roofed, half-walled, bus-sized vehicle with no wheels floated above the floor and silently stopped in front of them. The door opened and they proceeded to get in. There was no driver. After they sat down, the bus hovercraft, as they thought of it, started moving toward a large open door on the far side of the hanger, about half a mile away. Astonishment was written across everyone's faces as they passed by ship after ship. Proceeding through the next doorway, they came to a stop just outside the hanger opening and were asked to get off and stand on one of the many pads on the floor by the wall. They were advised to close their eyes till they felt the bright light subside.

When the nine guests opened their eyes, they could see they were in a much smaller sitting area. The area seemed as if it had been designed just for them. There was a half-moon conference-sized table in front of them with exactly nine office chairs on their side of it. There were jugs of what looked like water and glasses on the table in front of each chair. About twenty feet in front of this table was a raised platform, maybe twelve inches high, with a similar table and only six chairs behind it. The group decided to sit at the table and have some water; they were thirsty after the journey and all the excitement they felt from it.

The nine had only been seated for about two minutes when a door materialized behind the other table and in walked two men, both over six feet tall, followed by two women and two other men.

Mr. White and Mr. Brown sat in the chairs on each end of the table, leaving the four chairs in the middle for Donna, Sam, Nathan, and Claire. Sam remained standing when the others sat. He understood the psychology of having their table higher than the table for the nine. He also understood he had to take control of this meeting right from the start.

"Welcome, gentleman and lady. My name is Sam White and it is I who have asked you all here. I don't need to know your names or any other information about your lives. I am fully aware of how your organization operates. I am also aware of all the corporations you control. Your power is the main reason we asked you all here."

Several of the nine individuals started to ask questions at the same time. Sam responded by pounding his fist once on the table. He looked straight at them and said, "We are not here to hurt you physically or condemn your organizations. We brought you here to inform you that your past actions have put Earth in a very bad position and discuss what we must do to rectify this situation."

One of the nine stood up and asked, "And just how do you know who we are and what we have done or not done in the past? How dare you judge us"!

Very firmly, Sam said, "Sit down." The man slowly sat as requested, becoming silent. He knew he had to stay quiet till at least he found out all that was going on here. But he had no intention of taking the blame for Earth's problems. He personally felt his group made Earth a better place to live. So what if they got rich doing it.

Sam decided to give them some of his background and an idea of where this meeting was headed. "We, sitting at this table, are made up of two groups. The two gentlemen at the ends of the table are from a planet called Atlantica. You nine are sitting inside one of their Atlantis Galaxy Class ships."

Sam's audience was taken aback by the name "Atlantis." They had always thought the term referred to a myth; as such, it was not important to their aspirations on Earth.

Sam continued. "As for the four of us sitting in the centre, two of us—he pointed at Nathan and Claire—are also from Atlantica but have lived on Earth for many years gathering information. This information, by the way, is what has brought each and every one of us in this room together. Beside me here," he pointed at Donna, "is my wife, Donna. We were both born on Earth and died there. If you check records, you will learn who we were."

One of the nine, the woman, stood up. She asked, "If both of you died on Earth, what are you doing here now? Is there an afterlife?"

Sam answered, "Your question is of no concern at this time." "I just wanted you all to know that we are both human and lived our lives on Earth, therefore we can emphasize with its problems from its perspective. We learned many disturbing things, even in our short lifetimes, about how the greed of the few got us to this point in time."

"How can you call what we do 'greed'? We, all of us," she said, pointing at the other eight, "have worked very hard to get where we are today. Man's goal is to work hard and try to achieve greatness in a lifetime. What is so wrong with that?"

Sam smiled at the way these people defended everything they did and twisted the truth to make their actions sound morally acceptable. He said, "Okay, here is a short list for you all to ponder. By mentioning just a few things here, we want you to realize we are aware of your group and its scope. By getting to know each other better, I feel it will be easier to move forward with our goal.

"We know your organization consists of millions of people. The people in the upper part know that only a few on top control things. Then we go downwards in the organization all the way to the rice farmer in China and the housewife in Kansas who know absolutely nothing of your organization. But they know inside that they are all paying a higher price to live than they should be. They feel it in their guts; each and every day they struggle just to make a living, to house, clothe, and feed their children. They know you exist, they just don't have your names. They know that if they speak loud enough and often enough they will be called conspiracy nuts and shunned. So they shut up and continue doing things as they have always done to put food on the table.

"Let me say up front, I do not wish to sound condescending toward any of you. I know you are all very skilled business people and have worked hard to achieve your status. However, you nine have helped create, through your industrialization of nations without concern for the environment, CO_2 emissions at historic highs. From 1850 until today, CO_2 emissions have climbed over twenty-five percent globally. The use of fossil fuels without proper controls has led to seventy-two percent of this increase. In the atmosphere there is a CO_2 concentration of four hundred and twenty-five ppm (parts per million). In terms a normal person can understand, this is equal to an average of four tons of CO_2 production per person globally per year. The industrialized nations on Earth are averaging eleven tons per person. There has also been an increase in world temperatures in the range of three to five degrees Celsius.

"The world's population is now seven and a half billion. Over the next hundred years the poorer nations will start to industrialize and the world population will rise. What the new statistics will be by that time is anybody's guess.

"Many people on Earth are aware that inventions and discoveries in the past and even today have been bought up and hidden from them. This includes inventions that would greatly reduce the amount of gasses warming the earth. In the process of making your billions, you have set the Earth on a collision course with its own death."

"On one hand, you can say this is not your fault; governments should have done better with their regulations. But we also know that money from special interest groups makes it into the hands of governments and makes any regulations easier to get past.

"My group also understands that the emissions from factories, autos, and power generation stations are not the whole cause of global warming. Let me tell you some facts about CO_2 emissions. All the factories on earth together are dumping approximately six billion tons of CO_2 per year into the atmosphere. Is this bad? It sure as hell is. But even a single solitary volcano, which can pump out over fifty million tons of carbon monoxide into the atmosphere in a single day, also contributes. There are at least a dozen volcanoes, big and small, on land and under the oceans, erupting regularly. At this time you have no control over these. CO_2 levels this high, no matter the cause, are unacceptable. This problem needs to be attended to today, not tomorrow."

The nine sat silently. They all knew this Sam guy in front of them was a pretty smart cookie. "Your group is making billions off this issue, in solar panels, wind farms, and ocean tide turbines, just to name a few. You know the levels of emissions are still on the rise, even with all the money governments put into reductions. Smart business people like yourselves know that if you want to make money on something, you create a shortage in one area while being the supplier of the alternative in another area: business 101.

"The Earth also has its own cycles of global warming and cooling. Have you all even taken a second to realize the Earth has a very carefully balanced ecosystem and maybe, just maybe, everyone should start asking why it is getting out of balance with itself?

"Moving on," Sam said, "We here at this table know, as I said at the beginning, that your group has some control over almost every country on Earth. You are the ones who inform countries where and when to start industrialization. You tell governments which third world nations should build factories because their pollution standards are so much less aggressive than those of other nations. Your insistent need for power and money and nothing-else-matters attitude is a big part of the problem. Take just one look at what you call the Middle East. Your group has tried several times to get full and utter control of this region because of the natural resources accumulated there. Each and every one of those schemes, and the manipulation of governments, has brought your world to the brink of another world war. Are you all incapable of seeing past your own noses?"

"Man was not placed on this Earth a hundred thousand years ago to help you achieve your goals or help you devise them. Man was put here to help the planet survive and become a more complete living organism. Yes, you heard me right: a living, breathing organism, just like you."

One of the men asked Sam if he could have a few minutes alone with his group. Sam said, "Not yet, please! I do not want any sidebars here. There can be no negotiating the facts. You were asked to come here for a reason, and we hope to come to agreement and consensus on the road we will all travel together. Until we reach an agreement, you will each be given a private suite aboard this ship, where you will be taken care of very, very well. Tomorrow night you will be given a conference room in which to speak amongst yourselves. After that, the only time you will be together again is when we meet in this room for more discussions. No, you are not prisoners. Consider yourselves our esteemed guests; you will be treated as such for your entire stay. Each of you will be escorted to your suite by a person we call 'Mr. White'; he will see to all your individual needs." The lights brightened and Sam and his group left the room.

By themselves in the cafeteria, Sam and his group compared notes. Sam said to his partners, "It all seems to be going well. I knew I had to knock them off their game by being the one to take control— something these nine have usually always had." Donna agreed, telling Sam that she was happy she got some of his memories on the trip; they helped her realize even more about what Sam had spoken of in his speech. Nathan spoke up and asked Sam if he thought he might have pushed too hard, it being a first meeting and all. Claire wondered the same, then looked at Nathan and smiled.

"I am hoping there was just enough firmness in my speech to start them thinking," Sam answered. "Maybe they will be more receptive at tomorrow's meeting. I did deviate from our plan a bit in talking so much about the environment and their involvement with it. I just wanted them to see, as I have, that if you do even a little thing in the right direction, improvements can happen."

Everyone at the table conceded that Sam was probably correct with his assessment. Nathan jumped up and said, "Enough, I am starving. Let's eat."

Sam picked the prime rib with mashed potatoes smothered in gravy; Donna got herself a chicken noodle soup with a ham sandwich. Nathan and Claire settled on big juicy cheeseburgers with fries. They sat and ate their meals, saying nothing more, though they all thought about the meeting tomorrow. Mr. White and Mr. Brown sat and watched them eat.

●　　　　●　　　　●

The next meeting got started at ten a.m. sharp. Both parties were seated in the same spots as yesterday. Sam started by asking if anyone had questions from yesterday. One man stood and asked Sam about the placing of humans on Earth so long ago and where they originally came from and why.

"Without going into too much detail," Sam said, "I told you about how the Earth is an actual living organism and needs balance to survive. Well, it just so happens that putting people here gave the Earth almost a reason, if you will, to work harder. As if it enjoyed expanding its ecology and making a new species comfortable, allowing it to thrive and become at one with the planet. I know this all sounds kind of romantic—a planet having a relationship with one of the species on it—but I believe this to be true. As far as where the people come from, they came from other more populated planets in the universe. This seeding of planets is the real goal of the people from Atlantica," Sam told him.

Sam nodded his head slightly and smiled, thanking the man for his thoughtful questions and telling him he was pleased that he had been listening yesterday. Another of the nine asked Sam why they were brought here. Sam said, "I would have thought you all might have guessed the answer to that one by now." He smiled.

"You will learn from us; we can help you with some of Earth's problems, just as you nine can help us get our message across to the people of Earth. We are here to help the Earth and its people, not take it over. After all," Sam said, "this is how your whole organization works, from the top on down. You have your ways of getting people to believe your corporations want to help them, all the while telling them what they need and how much they need to have happy lives. It will be your group's connections that will open the doors to all the leaders of your world and let them know we are here to help, not interfere.

"All I can tell you right now is, Earth needs our intervention and help from all the world's people as a united group. Without their help, the consequences will be very dire. Let me ask you, would threatening you change the direction the world is headed? Could all the money on Earth save a dying planet? All of you had better give your heads a shake and wake up to the new reality; it will be here sooner than you think."

The third gentleman from the right stood up and asked, "How are we to trust that what you are saying is the truth and that you are not here to take over and get everything for yourselves?"

Sam stood up slowly and calmly said, "I guess today's meeting is going to be very short. Before we leave, though, here is one more thought for you nine to ponder overnight. You have seen the size of this ship and some of its many technological wonders. Do you even think for a single second that we could not make happen what needs to be done for the Earth without your assistance? Do not take this statement as a threat in any way. We here on this ship believe getting the help of the people on a planet far outweighs the damage caused by going full steam ahead with no cooperative consideration. We want you to know that we are resolute in our plan to help and that failure is not an option. We want you all to be a part of this process. Meeting adjourned," Sam said abruptly.

Later on, alone in their suite, Donna hugged Sam as tears smeared her vision. She told him, "I am so angry with those people and their narrow-mindedness I could choke the whole lot."

"I feel the same way, Donna. I hope they think really hard about all I said."

The nine, alone in their own conference room, talked about everything Sam had said to them. Some came to the conclusion that Sam was right; he could just go ahead and do what he wanted to Earth: who would be able to stop him? Over the evening, they pretty much came to the conclusion that they would have to agree to working with Sam. They knew their way of life was going to change; all the ways they did things were going to be shaken to their foundations. After all, they had been the designers of change until now, though not necessarily the accepters of it. Most thought that perhaps their group had gone too far in not taking the health of the planet into consideration.

Early the next morning Sam was surprised; seven of the nine members asked to speak to him in private before the morning meeting. Mr. White moved the day's meeting to noon instead of ten a.m. and Sam made the rounds from one room to the next over the next three hours. Through the private meetings, Sam learned that these people did have a conscience; they did not think money was the end-all, be-all of life. In their own ways, they told Sam he was pretty much one-hundred-percent correct in every item he blamed them for. These seven agreed to support Sam; they too wanted a better Earth.

Just as he finished his last private meeting, the other two members of the group also asked for his presence in their rooms. Sam found that these two would never listen; all they were concerned with was what was in supporting Sam for them. Leaving the last of the nine, Sam got together with his team and filled them in on recent events. None of his team was surprised by the lack of support from the two men Sam mentioned. They agreed that seven was a lucky number; with the participation of that many, their plan would still work.

At noon, Sam had the two men who had refused to contribute willingly removed to their rooms, telling them that their support was not required. Maybe the other seven would figure out what to do with them when they returned to Earth; he washed his hands of the pair. In front of his team, Sam asked the remaining seven members to raise their hands if they were in support of making Earth a better place, telling them there would be no turning back. All seven raised their hands.

Sam was not fully aware of how the contacts of these individuals worked their magic and told them he was not concerned. They could have their secrets; he had some of his own. Sam was asked what technologies would be used on Earth. He named off a few from the top of his head; most of the terms gave the seven an idea of what each one did but no clue about how they did it. These were some of Sam's secrets.

Over the next several days, Sam gave the seven members a flex- ible timeline as to just how much information was to be given to the media and governments. This included the issue of how the mem- ber's in-pocket scientists would release the information about a ship arriving from space and make sure leaders had no reason to be frightened of the visitors. The seven went to work, making contact with everyone who could get the message across to all the people of Earth.

With the carefully-planned release of the news that there was life out there in space and that it was coming toward them, the people of Earth became gradually acclimatized to the idea of alien contact over the next several months. The world's scientists reassured them. There was even a message from the Pope; things would be okay with the arrival of the alien ship. Public hysteria was kept to a minimum, except, of course, for the crazies; they relished the idea of getting media coverage.

The seven members were allowed full speaking privileges with all their contacts on Earth. It was like they were orchestrating a choir; they were damn good, Sam thought. The two who had been unco-operative had been sent back to Earth with their memories wiped two months ago. Sam and his team thought the other seven would also need to have their memories wiped, but Donna told Sam she thought wiping was unfair; the seven were changed and had worked very hard to make Atlantis's arrival more pleasant for them. At some level, Sam had to agree with Donna, and finally told her they could retain their memories.

The day finally came. Sam ordered the captain of this ship, Captain Rogers, to proceed to Earth at a slower-than-usual pace and settle in orbit twenty-eight thousand miles up. They arrived in orbit within hours. All the nations' leaders were hailed in their own lan-guages. The message read, "Greetings from the Atlantis Class Galaxy ship Excelsior. We mean no harm and in no way will we be aggres-sive. The purpose of our journey here is to meet the people of Earth and share cultures with one another. We also wish to meet with the heads of every country on your fair planet to discuss matters ben-eficial to both of us. Please, take your time and respond when ready."

Sam knew his message would be picked up by NASA and army and navy bases around the globe. It was not long before most of the people on Earth were aware that an alien ship had arrived and was sitting in Earth's high orbit, awaiting a reply to its message.

There was no end to the amount of speculation. There were only a few—tens of thousands—who tried to push their own agendas through narratives of how they were being invaded and would all become slaves or worse. Most of these claims went unadvertised, and only a few actually made it into Earth's mainstream media. Sam could tell that the group of seven was able, for the most part, to quash most of this nonsense with their networks of influence.

Basically, the people of Earth were waiting for their governments to respond. Many were hoping change was about to happen: change for the betterment of mankind. It took the President of the United States just over three days to send a reply. "To the beings in the ship orbiting Earth," the President began, "I am John Watson, the leader of only one of the Nations here on Earth, but I speak for all." Sam surmised that a very quick consortium of the major nations had drafted this message together.

"We, the peoples of Earth, invite you, in peace and with open arms, in the hope of meeting on equal ground, to discuss the reasons you have come here. If you are true to your first message, saying you come in peace, we are very pleased. If not, the countries of our world are prepared to defend ourselves with every means at our disposal. If your intentions are peaceful, you are free to bring your ship down and land here on Earth."

Every nation had put their forces on high alert and mobilized everything in their arsenals. Sam and his group took the President's message as a positive first step in their arrival. Sam ordered Captain Rogers to land the ship in the exact spot it had landed some thirty-six hundred years ago, on the Sargasso Sea. This sea was in the centre of the Atlantic Ocean. Sam was always amazed by this: a sea in the middle of an ocean.

Sam told the captain he first wanted the ship to slowly pass over the United States at five miles high; he wanted people to see the size of the ship before touchdown in the Atlantic. The ship came down just outside the west coast and proceeded slowly, at about two hundred and fifty miles per hour, across the U.S. Sam was very sure the sight of his ship caused a lot of commotion and even some minor havoc on the ground. Having passed over Washington now, with several fighter jets and, at times, naval helicopters in tow, the ship headed to the middle of the Atlantic, where it landed on the surface of the water with barely a ripple.

Sam was home again. Now, he thought, the hard work starts. Sam had a message sent to the other forty ships, telling them to head toward Earth using Stealth Mode and stay behind the moon till needed. The message was received and acknowledged. It would take the other ships about two months to arrive.

Chapter 7
New Day

From the Excelsior, Captain Rogers broadcast a worldwide radio message that there would be a three-hundred-mile no-entry zone around his ship. The ship would be using its shields, which extended in a radius of one hundred and fifty miles and a height of ten miles. The other one hundred and fifty miles was a safety margin, in case any of Earth's planes or vessels got off course for any reason. The message let the people of Earth know that if any of their planes or vessels came in contact with this shield, they would be destroyed. The leaders of Earth agreed to these guidelines; they did the same thing when it was prudent to do so (such as when they held ground or naval exercises).

Sam and his team arranged for a first historic meeting on Earth's home ground. Sam asked if, for now, the meeting could be limited to the leaders of the major influential countries and their U.N. delegates. They were told interpreters would not be necessary. A few leaders questioned how the beings on the ship knew the names of all their countries but then realized they would not have come here without some kind of prior recon of Earth. All agreed to this meeting and a date and location was set for four days from now.

The Excelsior was informed that all security would be provided by the hosting nation: the United States. The meeting was to be in Washington at the White House. Sitting down with his team, Sam reminded them about his lack of taste for politics. They laughed at him, "poor baby!" they all said. Sam laughed with them.

The day arrived; Sam and his team flew in on a shuttle. The people of the world watched every second of their arrival on their TVs. The National Guard held back the crowd of hundreds of thousands of people on site. Almost every media outlet on the planet was present. The crowd was excited yet calm. No one was sure what was going to happen next.

The shuttle slowly flew over the city and came to a complete stop above and beside the White House. It hovered about three hundred feet from the ground. A door opened on the bottom of the ship and a large round, flat disc descended slowly to the ground. The crowd leaned forward for a better look as a beam of light came out of the bottom centre of the shuttle and up from the disc before meeting in the middle. Seconds later, as the light's intensity started to fade, everyone saw six human figures standing on the disc.

The media cameras zoomed in, capturing all their faces and broadcasting them worldwide. Just after what, to the viewers, looked like being beamed down, the cameras switched to the entrance of the White House. The President and First Lady walked out onto the terrace to greet their guests. Sam and his team climbed the steps to the terrace, walking over to the President. Members of the Secret Service moved in between the President and his guests. The President raised his hand and warded them off, telling them to stand down. With reluctance, they followed the order from their chief and commander and backed away.

The President reached out his hand; Sam took it and shook it firmly. "Greetings from the people of Earth," the President said. He was kind of puzzled; his guests all looked human. The shuttle lifted silently higher in the sky, then turned and sped away, leaving the disc.

Still holding the President's hand, Sam said, "Maybe we should go inside." He smiled.

The President smiled back. "Sounds good to me," he said. Sam and his team and the President and First Lady faced the crowd for a few seconds and waved before turning to go. The crowd let out a roar and started clapping as the entourage disappeared inside.

Once inside, introductions were made all around. Sam told the President and First Lady that he and Donna were from Earth. At this juncture, the First Lady excused herself and left the group. The President asked for Sam and his team to come with him. They walked into a small room and closed the door. The President typed his passcode into a panel on the wall and the whole room started to descend. President Watson informed Sam that they were going down over six hundred feet to the conference room. Not too many people in the world knew of this room. Some had speculated over the years, but no one could ever prove it existed.

When the room stopped descending, the President opened the door onto a long wide hallway leading to another door some hundred feet away. On both sides of the hall every twenty feet or so, stood Marines with holstered side arms.

The door was opened from inside and they all proceeded though it. Sam looked about the room; it was very large, with other doors along the walls. There was a huge table—maybe sixty feet long and ten feet wide—in the centre. Around it were several dozen comfortable office chairs. In the centre of the table was the emblem of the United States President's Office. The U.N. delegates sat in chairs along the walls. The heads of all the nations he had asked to be here—no one else—sat in the chairs around the table. Sam's team took seats on the side of the table opposite the leaders.

President Watson sat at the head of the table. He spoke first. "Perhaps we should all introduce ourselves before we start." The Japanese leader stood up and said, "I can understand every word you are saying; how are you doing this?" Some of the other members also spoke up. Everyone could hear in their native language; when their words came out, they were also heard by everyone in their own languages. The president was as confused as anyone; you could see it in his face.

Sam raised his hand. "Excuse me, gentlemen," he said loudly.

The leaders stopped talking and sat back. Sam stood up, looked at President Watson, and said, "If I may explain, sir."

The President answered, "By all means, please do."

Sam asked Mr. White to reveal the device clipped to his inside jacket pocket. Everyone leaned forward to see an apparatus no bigger than a cell phone hanging from Mr. White's pocket. Sam told the group this was a Universal Translator and could automatically take all languages and translate them. "This way," Sam said, "There will be no confusion as to what is said here, each person could speak their own language and it would be understood by all others."

The leader of Russia said, "Very well. We could use some of those around here." Everyone laughed and the tension slid down several notches. Still standing, Sam pointed to the different people in his team and introduced them.

President Watson asked several questions about Sam and Donna's involvement with aliens from space. They gave the President and the rest a full accounting of where they were born, their families here, how their lives had ended, and why they were asked, upon rejuvenation on Atlantica, to come speak to the people of Earth about a crisis in the making.

Sam said, "My team and I are not here to take you over or cause harm in any way. Our goal is to sit down with you, and eventually all the people of Earth, to work on a solution to the coming crisis. I will tell you all right now that you will not be lied to or manipulated in any way. My team and I will tell you what the crisis is. We will work in conjunction with all of Earth's resources, technologies, and people. We will bring in extra resources and technologies of our own to help solve this crisis.

"My team and I will not get involved in your politics, religions or petty squabbles here on Earth. We have a much bigger job to do and do not need, pardon me, any bullshit or lies from special interest groups. Groups, I might add, that have already manipulated departments in almost every government on this planet to fill their own pockets, doing the wrong things for the planet and its people.

"Please, take a few minutes to really think about all I have just said. And—two more little things—first, my team will not keep secrets, except about our technologies, from you. You are not ready yet for most of these technologies. Second, every single human being on this planet will eventually be brought up to speed on every aspect of our proposals and the solutions we arrive at in our meetings." Looking at President Watson, Sam said, "A government for the people, by the people." He sat down.

Everyone in the room sat back. They looked at each other for several seconds, then a bombardment of questions came Sam's way. The men in this room knew politics and proper meeting decorum; one person at a time or mayhem.

President Watson asked the first question. "What is this crisis you spoke of?" Sam appreciated the directness and brevity of the question. Right to the point, he thought. Over the next few hours, Sam's team laid out everything they knew about the crisis for the leaders. They even began some talks on possible solutions for resolving it.

Once the problems were laid out in front of them, the leaders slowly came around to a consensus: every nation on the planet would have to work together. This, they all knew, was going to be almost impossible to accomplish. They were well aware of their political differences and the petty squabbles, as Sam called them, between them.

Nearing the end of the meeting, Sam spoke once more to the leaders. "When I was growing up, my father told me an old saying: 'United we stand, divided we fall.' Perhaps that is an analogy we can use today?"

President Watson spoke to the group. "Well, there you have it, gentlemen. We either stop all the crap going on here on Earth or we will lose it."

"Can we afford to keep playing the same old games and maybe lose everything?" the leader of Japan asked. He, for one, wanted to hear more from Sam's team and felt a vote should be taken to confirm that everyone was in agreement. They all raised their hands. It was too early to discuss anything with their respective governments till they heard more.

The next meeting was scheduled for the following day at ten a.m., this time on Sam's ship, the Excelsior. Sam told the delegates he would send a shuttle to pick them up. The group of leaders was in full agreement; they wanted to see his ship.

Sam and his team left the White House, boarded the shuttle, and returned to the ship. The leaders stayed put in the conference room. Mr. White left the voice translator device on the table before he left, telling them they could bring it to the next meeting. He told the group, "Please do not play with it or try to open it. The device would turn itself off and the internal workings would disintegrate."

Once back on board the Excelsior, Sam told the captain about tomorrow's meeting onboard and asked that a room, refreshments, and accommodations be set up for the foreign leaders. Captain Rogers told Sam that all would be ready and that he would send his own, Captains shuttle to pick them up.

For the rest of the evening the team talked amongst themselves; they all felt like some headway had been made today. They came up with a game plan for tomorrow. Sam told his team they would have to do something special tomorrow and let the leaders be a part of it; he hoped it would help convince them that his team was here for the good of mankind. Nathan asked what Sam had in mind. Sam just smiled and was silent. The others gave up; all they wanted now was a bite to eat, a few drinks, and sleep. It had been a very hectic day.

●

●   ●

At nine a.m. sharp, the Captain's shuttle went through the shield and headed to Washington. The leaders were all waiting on the lawn. They were picked up and taken to the ship. Media around the globe reported every second of what went on. Most of the reports were favourable. Overnight, ceasefires had been ordered around the world. Riots stopped and people missed work to catch the latest report. The world was listening and waiting.

As the shuttle got closer to the ship, many of the leaders asked the Mr. White onboard about the Excelsior's size, how it flew silently and could travel in both space and Earth's atmosphere, what kind of propulsion engines it had, and how fast it could go. The questions went on and on. Mr. White told them it was not up to him, but to Sam and his team, to fill them in.

There were at least ten fighter jets or other planes keeping track of the shuttle till it crossed into the no-fly zone. The shuttle arrived at the Excelsior, came to a complete stop, and hovered silently. From the ship's roof, several doors opened and out came another fifty shuttles, rising to their level and hovering. The leaders wondered what was going on. Mr. White told them that Sam would be onboard their shuttle shortly.

Several minutes later, the door to the room where the leaders were opened and in walked Sam. "Good morning, gentlemen. I trust you all had a good night's sleep?" They nodded and then President Watson asked Sam what was happening. "Nothing right this second, but I wanted you to see a few of the many ways we can help Earth and make it a better place to live. Please have a seat and watch the view screen." Within seconds, the group saw their shuttle race across the United States and hover just over what looked like a huge fenced-in area.

"Where are we?" the President asked Sam. Sam informed him that they were now hovering over one of the fifty-four nuclear waste disposal sites the United States had created.

After about thirty seconds the shuttle accelerated and headed much higher into the sky. Before the leaders knew it, they were in space. President Watson asked how this was possible—how they got into space so fast yet felt nothing. Sam told him about the Inertial Dampening System on board the shuttle. He then said to the leaders, "Here, watch," as he pointed at the screen. They saw the sun come into view, getting bigger and bigger in mere seconds. A filter dropped down over the window so no one would be blinded.

The leaders were astonished; they were in space and flying toward the sun and it had only taken minutes. "We are close enough now," Sam said to the captain. The next thing everyone on board saw on the screen were hundreds of metal canisters flying toward the sun. "There you go," Sam said. "The entire waste storage from that site has now been safely eliminated."

All the President could say was, "That's fantastic. Thank you, Sam."

"You're welcome. That is not all. As we made the trip here, several other shuttles have traversed the globe and picked up material from other nuclear waste sites in various countries. They've sent it all into the sun. This process will take about four days to finish. There are also a few shuttles flying around the Earth in your orbiting zone, picking up every piece of space junk your ships and astronauts let get away from them. There should be no more need for you to waste resources trying to track each piece."

The leaders all clapped. The Canadian delegate said, "You have just done—in hours—what would have taken over half a million years to accomplish, with the nuclear waste, and decades, with cleaning up the junk in orbit! Bravo!"

Sam spoke. "Now we will return to Atlantis for today's meeting and some refreshments." The shuttle headed back to the Excelsior and docked inside. The leaders were escorted to the conference room.

Sam knew many people on Earth had seen the shuttles he sent out and asked his group of seven to make sure the news wires got hold of the information about just what they were doing. A few of the countries had shot at some of the shuttles in their air space. Sam was not concerned; the shuttles had shields.

At his table, Sam stood. "As you have seen, we did not take politics or boundaries into consideration to accomplish this necessary task. We saw a problem, figured out what needed to be done, and did it. The world just became a tiny bit safer. No one was harmed in this process; all that happened was the illegal crossing of borders and infringement on air space."

The leader from Great Britain stood. "Just what are your plans for Earth and its people?" Sam sat down and passed the floor to Donna.

Donna stood and looked at all the leaders. "Gentlemen, we have only been here for a few days and have already made some very slight progress. Thus far you have learned who we are and where we are from. You have learned that an Atlantis ship was here two times in the past hundred thousand years. You have also learned that sometimes taking an action where there was none before might be the right thing to do. Attempts to find a solution to the problems here on Earth have been made for a very long time, yet these problems are still there and getting bigger. We, here on this side of the table, have some knowledge as to why these problems came about, but it is in no one's interest to play a blame game. You here in this room are leaders—the ones the people of Earth look to for support and guidance. None of you got to where you are by being frivolous with your ideals.

"Let me apologize for what may seem like a long speech. I hope you don't feel that I'm treating you like children; this is not the message I want to get across. I am trying to make sure you understand; it is time to stop the proliferation of small problems before they get too big—like the ones you are having now. Any solutions we, as a group, come up with in this room will be just the tip of the iceberg. For every solution, there will be anywhere from hours of discussion to years of negotiation. You all know change takes time. We know consultation with each and every level of your governments and your people has to come before decisions can be made. I and my team will tell you here and now that we are willing to stand at your sides through all the changes that need to happen.

"You should also know that if changes are not made soon, time will run out for all of us." Donna looked at Sam. He smiled at her, letting her know he was proud of her. "To answer to your question," Donna said, "We do have some plans made already. Some are fluid and may be changed along the way and some are firm, in order for all this effort to have lasting effects. We want, at this time, to send you back to your respective nations, where you will begin talks with your people. Find out what they feel should be done to make Earth a better place to live. Would it be safe to allot perhaps three to four months for this stage?"

The leader of China replied, "That amount of time should be workable." He looked at his colleagues for confirmation. A majority nodded their heads.

Sam thought, Speak to Cube. The voice asked Sam how things were going. As of this time, we have found some consensus. The leaders of Earth are willing to work with us, and I think this is a good first step so early. The voice agreed and thanked Sam for the update.

•   •   •

Over the next several weeks, the shuttles were able to complete the work of cleaning up the space debris and nuclear waste. Sam's team went over their timelines again, tweaking expectations here and there. At this point, Nathan mentioned to Sam that he was not so sure about speaking about some of the more trivial matters facing the Earth when it was his turn to speak to the people. These matters he was to speak of were hinging on interference in earths affairs, such as legal, moral and political issues. He felt these issues might become a distraction when they were trying to get the people to see the bigger picture. Sam explained to Nathan that sometimes it was also important to speak of the little things; they also had an effect on the outcome of the bigger picture they were going to present.

Sam went on in his explanation. He felt that if they only spoke about the main problems and relayed to the people just how big these problems were—without giving some small hope to the people with regard to less significant issues—they might not get them on their side. Sam told Nathan that this would be a tricky balancing act but that Sam believed he could do it. Nathan relented and said he would give it his best shot.

The bottom line, or big picture, in their plan was to have at least four billion of the seven and a half billion people on Earth moved to other planets in the universe and to begin implementing new technologies which would help instigate repairs to Earth's ecosystem.

The leaders found speaking to their governments a daunting task, to say the least. Making changes to allow public knowledge of just what they wanted to do and how they were going to do it was also a gargantuan task. The move to transparency was a significant shift from the way they had previously operated, which had entailed keeping many secrets from the people.

As for the people, they were enjoying their new ability to speak to their governments and have what they were saying actually listened to. It was hard for them to accept change after centuries of lies and deceit by their leaders. The existence of the Atlantis ship, sitting in the ocean, had begun to be accepted and cause less excitement. The people were starting to understand there was more in their existence than just themselves.

Sam and his team were notified by various governments about riots and uprisings against change. The team did not spend a lot of time together over these few months; they were spread out around the globe, standing with various leaders, explaining why they had come and why it was time to embrace change. Sam came to realize his team was too small to be everywhere.

A decision was made to bring things up a notch. By this time, Atlantica's ships had all arrived and were stationary behind the moon. Sam informed all the national governments that he was going to bring another forty Galaxy Class ships into Earth's orbit to help get their message across. At first, many of the leaders voiced their concerns about this action, saying that it would frighten their people into thinking they were now going to be attacked. Sam explained why more help was necessary and the leaders came to a fuller understanding. They knew time was of the essence; information about everything happening since Atlantis's arrival was not getting out to all the people fast enough.

The forty ships took up a gyro-synchronistic orbit around Earth. At the agreed-upon time, a nontoxic gas was released into the atmosphere. This gas formed a thin cloud layer around the entire planet. This cloud cover, sixty thousand feet above the surface of the Earth, was dense enough and stable enough to allow screen-quality transmissions to be displayed on it. In total, there was now over one hundred thousand screens of enormous size covering the entire inside of the cloud cover.

No matter where people lived, they could see at least one or two of the screens. Night and day around the planet was taken into account for picture clarity. Each of Earth's 297 languages and all its dialects were taken into account as well. In this way, what was shown and discussed would be understood by all people at the same time.

This was a technology Atlantica had developed for just this type of scenario. The time of the transmission was broadcast to all the countries of the world. Sam's team had arranged for this broadcast to come from the top deck of the Excelsior. At the prescribed time all the screens were activated and the first around-the-globe broadcast showed a small round dot in the middle of the Atlantic Ocean. Slowly the picture focused inward toward the top of the ship. As it zoomed in, everyone could see just how big the ship was. They could now see the flotilla of ships come into view all around the Excelsior, about three hundred miles away. Huge naval vessels such as aircraft carriers and destroyers looked puny in comparison. The picture zoomed in until the viewer could make out a huge stage area on top of the ship, with hundreds of people sitting on chairs and a podium with a large table and a few chairs behind it.

The screens flickered for a second, then a frontal view of the head table came into view. Behind this table were hundreds of nations' flags, in miniature, flying on poles maybe twelve feet high. The world could now see Sam and his team at the head table, smiling and waving toward the camera. After a moment their hands all came down; they placed them on the tabletop. To the world, they looked human, except for the ones on each end, who looked like some kind of twins (but with different hair colors).

Sam stood. "Welcome to my ship, the Excelsior. Please forgive us if getting to this point in time has frightened any of you in any way. Our arrival was never intended to be seen as a threat. The reason for this worldwide broadcast is to enable you, the people of Earth, to see and hear first-hand why we came here. We have spoken in private to all your leaders over the past several months. We came to the same conclusion: you, the people, were not getting your questions answered quickly enough. We, from Atlantica, wish to tell you that in general you have elected your leaders very well, in our opinion. Each and every one of them has seen and heard why we are here. However, their messages to you have not come across very well at all times; hence this broadcast.

"Most of your leaders are sitting here on this deck with me and my team. The ones who are here all show support for our plans and the goals we must achieve to make your Earth a better place to live. You may be thinking, at this point, Who are you to come to our planet and tell us how to make our world better? I can answer this question with," pointing at Donna, "My wife, Donna and I are from Earth; we lived our entire lives here and are therefore very aware of its problems, just as you all are. The other four members of our team are from Atlantica, and have also been to Earth in the past."

"Now I will get to what we and your leaders all feel is the problem. The Earth you live on is only one of millions of such planets in this galaxy alone; there are millions upon millions more in the universe. You are not alone. You are not special, but you are unique. By this I mean that yours is one of the Worlds becoming overpopulated. Does this mean we have to kill vast numbers to get the population down? No. Killing is not an option. Life is too important and fragile.

"It is because of the size of your population and its effect on the planet's ecosystem—which balances life on this world—that we have to take steps to heal the Earth. 'Heal,' because your world has become sick; there is every possibility it could die from its illness. If this were to happen, you would also all die. Forgive my bluntness; what I am saying has to be said. Let us take a little trip back in Earth's history.

"For more than two hundred and sixty million years, dinosaurs roamed the earth. They were everywhere. There were billions upon billions of their kind, eating, killing, and dying of old age. But no matter how many died or were killed, even greater numbers were born. Even then, the world, had limits on how many beings could populate its surface.

"What I am about to tell you is going to sound farfetched and unbelievable but it is the truth. The Earth became sick trying to house and feed a population of this size. It could not. Your world is a living, breathing organism and needed, at that point, to defend itself. It did. It tried to wipe out the illness. The earth defended itself with worsening weather and settled upon an ice age to solve its problem. Once most of the animal life was removed, it had time before the ice age retreated to heal itself and start over.

"Roughly one hundred thousand years ago, an Atlantis ship came to Earth with several hundred thousand humans from other planets. When these humans arrived, they carried with them the knowledge of Atlantica and its technologies. The Atlantis ship returned to Atlantica, leaving Earth seeded by enough humans to make their survival sustainable. These humans spread out over what you call the Middle East today. It was only about one hundred generations later that Atlantica and the Atlantis ship came to be considered a myth and then legend. Stories became less and less important with humans too busy just trying to survive.

"The stories of Atlantis all but disappeared for thousands of years but came to the forefront again after the second arrival of an Atlantis ship around thirty-seven hundred years ago. This new arrival was sent to check up on man's survival and see how the population was progressing.

"It was shortly after this arrival that I was born here on Earth. By this time, the world's population had grown to approximately three hundred million. People had migrated to all four corners of the Earth, for food, water, and better living conditions. The people of North and South America had been isolated from the rest of the world for some time after the ice bridge between Russia and Alaska collapsed.

"As you are aware, through your historical texts, Atlantis was in the middle of the Atlantic Ocean. Hundreds of its people spread out around the globe and passed on some of their knowledge and skills to the people of Earth.

"Was it wise or unwise to interfere in the people's development? Only you can surmise that. For better or worse, the Atlantis ship did not leave till man gained the knowledge of sea travel. Some of the ship's people decided to stay; they were told non-interference was to be their guide. As you are aware from your historians, this did not always work. So," Sam said, "now you have a history of our background. I will pass the baton, as you would say, to Nathan, one member of my team."

"Hello to all the people of Earth. Our team here has been trying our best to fill you and your leaders in on some of your history in the hopes that understanding where we are today will help you decide on a path for the future. I will tell you now about the first of a few of the technologies we are willing to supply the peoples of Earth.

"The first technology will be satellites, put in orbit to allow for better control of weather on this planet. Control of these satellites will remain in our hands for the time being. We will take direction from your leaders and their scientists and climatologists to make subtle changes to weather around the globe. We will work with you and try to alleviate the damage of some weather patterns—those that cause severe damage and hardships to people and their properties. This weather-controlling system is but a Band-Aid for the moment, to give Earth a more stable climate.

"Next, with your permission only, we will offer advice about a better way for handling your very worst career criminals—the people in your society who are genetically predisposed to murder, the killers who, for whatever reason, have no moral conscience. Those with no feeling of remorse whatsoever: sociopaths. We ourselves have come across such humans and know they can never be rehabilitated. Certain genes in their makeup are missing. The system we can bring in would place these criminals on another planet far from here. All their needs, such as shelter, the ability to grow their own food, and the tools to manage their own survival, would be taken care of. There would be no security needed; they would be left to their own devices. You, the people of Earth, would no longer have to pay for their activities through your taxes or personal safety. This, in turn, would free up some of your financial resources for rehabilitation of your lesser criminals.

"At the present time, there are over four hundred maximum-security prisons on your planet overflowing with the criminals from your societies. We believe that ninety-eight percent of these people can be rehabilitated and lead normal lives, benefitting mankind and themselves. We will not take it upon ourselves to mete out justice. That is the job of your criminal justice systems. We would just provide those systems an alternative. It will be your decision alone as to whether you are tired of putting criminals back on the streets of your cities only because your prisons are full and room needs to be made for new inmates. We are not judging your system of justice or what you do or do not do.

"The next step in this process would be the removal of any type of weapon used in the commission of a crime. The use of a weapon would give the perpetrator an immediate sentence of ten years in prison with zero deals allowed on this portion of sentencing. Then and only then would a sentence be given for the actual crime itself. A weapon could be defined as any external device that could cause physical harm—anything from a pin to an automatic handgun. We will leave this to your discretion. All weapons used in crimes would be destroyed after sentencing. Not going any further down this road, all I can say is we can supply several options to help with law and order if you so desire. Requests must come from your highest courts.

"If we can get this far, eventually, with the criminal justice system, then we can look at the weapons of mass destruction on your planet. This includes nuclear and hydrogen bombs and any nation's ability to use these types of weapons to cause harm to another nation. My team and I do not expect huge movement on any of these projects for years or, possibly, decades, but we hope that you will consider moving forward with them. I will now pass you to Sam's wife, Donna, to explain the next area in which we can assist your world, if requested."

"As a fellow human and the wife of a human," Donna started, "I can tell you, I am aware of the everyday struggles families have to make a living and care for their children. As the world's population grows, there are fewer jobs and less food. Some people who cannot find jobs revert to criminal activities to provide for themselves and their families. They don`t want to become criminals but they have run out of options and feel that doing something, even if it is illegal, is better than doing nothing. I do not have children but I have seen children neglected and going hungry, even in this day and age, when these conditions shouldn't exist. Our team is aware of this situation. At some point, most families wonder, what is the use of all this? My life is not getting better, no matter how much effort I put in to make it so.

"It can seem like a never-ending downward spiral into depression. What can you, as an individual, do? What you may not understand is that there are just too many humans on the planet for your governments to take care of. As my husband, Sam, said earlier, there are too many people on this planet for it to support. We are not here to tell you what to do; we can only tell you what must be done to bring balance back to the Earth. Without depressing you further, I will now pass you to Claire, Nathan's wife."

Claire stood. "I will try to be as straightforward and brief as I can. The conclusion this team and your leaders have come to is that the number of people on this planet needs to be reduced." Claire paused for a few seconds to let that statement sink in. "There are presently seven and a half billion people on earth. This number needs to be brought down to three billion. Meaning, four and a half billion people need to be relocated. 'How?' and 'Where to?' are the next questions. These questions are the ones we have been trying to get you to think about for the past several months. We hope the information we are providing will make your decisions easier to make.

"We, from Atlantica, are willing to provide relocation and support to all those who chose to be moved to other worlds—worlds not so different from Earth. Humans can survive very well on any of these planets; their climates and atmospheres are all almost identical to Earth's. We will also provide you with new goals to achieve. There would be no weapons or even governments to dictate to you how to live your lives. The only rules would be the ones you create for yourselves. Other than support for the first decade or so, settlers on these planets will be left alone to make new homes. All we ask is for you to try to make these better worlds. With the experiences you have from Earth and the problems you have overcome here, we know you are smart enough to succeed.

"We will also be staying on Earth to help the people who remain adjust and transform their lives into better ones, for their sakes and that of the planet. Each and every one of you—the ones who stay and the ones who move—will have another chance to improve your lives. It is now time to give you back to Sam, the leader of our team."

Sam began again. "I believe my team has laid out for you the foundation of why we are here and some of the things we can do for you. It will be up to you to decide what path to take; once again, though, I must stress the importance of time. We would like to see the people of the world thinking this over and making up their minds within the next year. No doubt, a change to your world has already begun, even with what you heard today. Many people will be anxious for change and others too afraid to start over. We do understand. Please take your time and make the right decision for you. I would now like to turn the floor over to the President of the United States."

President Watson addressed the world. "Citizens of Earth, I would like to remind you that change has never been easy. Choosing to start over again, perhaps losing everything of material value, will never be an simple choice. Ask your forefathers, who traversed an ocean to get here, leaving loved ones and their homes behind. Even within our own nation, settlers left the east coast and travelled with great hardship across the continent toward California. Reasons for doing so were as various as the people who took on the challenge.

We Americans are a strong breed, willing to take on new challenges and adventures; this is what has made us who we are today. Early peoples around the world migrated to all four corners of the globe; they too were afraid.

"All of us here on this planet must finally make a decision that will make both our survival and the survival of Earth achievable. I want to say to all of you, let us not look back and beat ourselves up for bad decisions or wrong moves in this game of life we enjoy so much. Let us hold our heads high, our faces stern into this wind of change. Let us beat it down into submission as we always have. Let us embrace this new reality and go forward, not turning back. Thank you."

After speeches to their own people and the world's people from several of the other leaders, the broadcast came to an end, leaving people to make their own decisions. The screens dissipated, along with the cloud cover. Earth was as it had been before.

Shuttles transported everyone onboard the ship back to their own countries. Sam and his team retired below deck. The Atlantis ship was alone again. "I believe we got our message across very well. What do all of you think?" Sam asked. The Mr. Whites and his team were in agreement.

The only comment was from Donna, who said, "I sure hope enough people make the decision to relocate." Everyone on the team just nodded their heads.

"Speak to Cube," Sam said when he was alone for a moment.

"Yes, Sam, nice to hear from you. How is it going?" Sam filled in the superiors. The voice told Sam he was pleased with his method of communication, talking to all at the same time.

Beyond helping Earth's people out with some of their minor issues along the way, the next step was on hold as they waited for decisions to be made about relocation to other worlds.

Chapter 8
The Time Has Come

A few weeks later, the team began receiving, from the various nations, the names of those who wished to relocate. The list of names was in the tens of thousands and multiplying quickly. Sam and his team were very pleased that the broadcast had the effect they hoped for. As each of the forty ships in orbit filled to capacity, the people who chose to relocate were told that, one at a time, the ships would leave orbit and take them to their new worlds.

It only took a month to get the first three million names. The shuttles travelled nonstop for over two weeks to fill the first ship. When boarding was complete, the captain asked permission from Sam to depart. Permission was granted and the ship departed for a planet far away in this galaxy. The fact that this planet was within the Milky Way would mean that the return trip would take less time. As more ships left, they went to other galaxies much farther away.

By the time the first year had passed, over two and a quarter billion people had started new lives on distant worlds. Support craft remained on these planets, allowing the larger ships to return to Earth.

Sam thought that the changes on Earth were progressing very well. The numbers of handguns and automatic weapons in the hands of gangs and criminals had been reduced drastically. Once the justice systems and governments adopted some of the new pro-cedures, criminals practically threw their weapons away, figuring on new ways of stealing or hurting people. The local police were more capable now, with fewer people on earth; tracking down and captur-ing criminals was much easier. Over time, Sam knew the numbers of police officers around the globe would dwindle, since crime would no longer be profitable enough for people to take the chance of getting caught.

As for big food businesses, there were fewer workers and fewer mouths to feed. Some of the higher-tech buildings were shut down and more people were put to work in smaller operations. It began to be a win—win situation for both owners and labourers. Employment numbers were at all-time highs and overhead costs for corporations came down. The same thing could be said for most other businesses on the planet.

As for weapons of mass destruction, the major leaders were almost at a final drafting stage to approve plans to have them all sent into the sun. Sam's team was ecstatic about the progress. Governments had more money in their coffers to repair infrastruc-ture, build more parks, and even demolish bad areas of entire cities. People were beginning to come back out of their homes and get to know their neighbours. They appeared to like the changes in their lives.

The gangs that used to roam the cities of the world started to become more involved with their communities in legal ways. There were more jobs than people and these members of society now felt they could make something of themselves and stay out of the jails. People were given birth rate numbers for family units to help keep the population in check. The people agreed and moved forward. The armies and navies of the world got much smaller.

When each Atlantis Class Galaxy ship landed on a new world, it stayed long enough for other support and supply vessels to arrive. In the meantime, people had a roof over their heads and three meals a day while they started to colonize their new home and begin farming for a food supply and building shelters. The people were extremely busy but they enjoyed every single minute of their lives on the new planets. They were told that Atlantica intended to end all involvement in their lives by the end of ten years. A time line and a goal: this is what humans needed to thrive.

By the end of year two, four and a half billion people had been seeded throughout the known universe. The population of Earth sat at just over three billion souls. The borders of many nations had come down and civil unrest was almost unheard of. With no need for huge armies and arsenals, money was used for building cleaner factories and cleaning up the waste of a thousand years of landfill sites.

The people were never told of the satellite in orbit around their worlds that gathered their auras upon their deaths; there was no need for them to know this information. Nor were they told that the moons orbiting their planets were power collectors and distributors for their worlds' future power usage.

Earth carried on with all its religions and politics and even started a few more. By the end of the fifth year of the Atlantis ship's arrival, so much progress had been made that Sam's team decided it was time for them to leave. Smaller vessels would return with a small contingent of Mr. Whites to make sure that if the people of Earth needed further assistance they would have it. They were on the right path and would remain that way far into the future.

The cube and its voice were now silent. Sam, Donna, Nathan, and Claire, along with Mr. White and Mr. Brown, returned to Atlantica and took their places amongst its citizenry. Sam and Donna learned everything they could about their new home.

One more huge surprise was on the way: Donna was pregnant! Over the next thousand years, Sam and Donna lived many more lives and adventures, and brought many children into existence. Nathan and Claire were always at their side, friends forever. Mr. White pushed forward and learned everything he could about humanity and even managed to mostly understand human feelings and thoughts. Sam was proud of him; he was now, in Sam's view, closer to being human than ever before.

Sam and Donna visited the many worlds they had seeded on several occasions to see the progress they had achieved. They were never happier.

In the wee hours of dawn one morning, centuries later, Sam was once again awakened by the voice from the cube...

THE END
... MAYBE

CPSIA information can be obtained at www.ICGtesting.com
Printed in the USA
LVOW07*1833300116

472383LV00004B/18/P